Planet
Earth
Is
Blue

PLANET EARTH IS BLUE

Nicole Panteleakos

WENDY
LAMB
BOOKS

Text copyright © 2019 by Nicole Panteleakos
Jacket art copyright © 2019 by Jungsuk Lee

All rights reserved. Published in the United States by Wendy Lamb Books, an imprint of Random House Children's Books, a division of Penguin Random House LLC, New York.

Wendy Lamb Books and the colophon are trademarks of Penguin Random House LLC.

"Space Oddity" Words and Music by David Bowie. © Copyright 1969 (Renewed) Onward Music Ltd., London, England. TRO Essex Music International, Inc., New York, controls all publication rights for the U.S.A. and Canada. International Copyright Secured. Made in U.S.A. All Rights Reserved Including Public Performance For Profit. Used by Permission.

Visit us on the Web! rhcbooks.com

Educators and librarians, for a variety of teaching tools, visit us at RHTeachersLibrarians.com

Library of Congress Cataloging-in-Publication Data
Names: Panteleakos, Nicole, author.
Title: Planet earth is blue / Nicole Panteleakos.
Description: First edition. | New York : Wendy Lamb Books, an imprint of Random House Children's Books, [2019] | Summary: Autistic and nearly nonverbal, twelve-year-old Nova is happy in her new foster home and school, but eagerly anticipates the 1986 Challenger launch, for which her sister, Bridget, promised to return. |
Identifiers: LCCN 2018022142 (print) | LCCN 2018028065 (ebook) | ISBN 978-0-525-64659-4 (ebook) | ISBN 978-0-525-64657-0 (trade) | ISBN 978-0-525-64658-7 (lib. bdg.)
Subjects: | CYAC: Sisters—Fiction. | Autism—Fiction. | Foster children—Fiction. | Middle schools—Fiction. | Schools—Fiction. | Challenger (Spacecraft)—Accidents—Fiction. | Space shuttles—Accidents—Fiction.
Classification: LCC PZ7.1.P35747 (ebook) | LCC PZ7.1.P35747 Pl 2019 (print) | DDC [Fic]—dc23

The text of this book is set in 13-point Bembo MT Pro.
Interior design by Trish Parcell

Printed in the United States of America
10 9 8 7 6 5 4 3
First Edition

Random House Children's Books
supports the First Amendment and celebrates the right to read.

— For —

Meadow & Brayden,

Kahliel & Caleb,

Jordyn, Josiah,

& Benjamin

Grown-ups never understand anything by themselves, and it is tiresome for children to be always and forever explaining things to them.

—Antoine de Saint-Exupéry, Le Petit Prince

Chapter One

Bridget was gone.

And Nova was broken.

Nova hadn't wanted to run away from the last foster family. They were nice enough. Sure, it wasn't easy sharing one bedroom with four other girls in three sets of bunk beds. There was no privacy for Bridget, who liked her space, and there was no room for hand flapping or bouncing, which Nova liked to do while pretending she was *in* space.

Plus there was a rule no shower could last more than eight minutes.

And they weren't allowed to watch TV, listen to records, or drink anything with caffeine.

But there had been hot oatmeal in the mornings. Cold lemonade with lunch. Warm blankets at night. Nobody yelled bad words or spanked them. Nobody made

Bridget scrub floors like Cinderella. Nobody called Nova Dumbo because she couldn't speak. Most importantly, they were together.

Bridget hated it anyway.

"I'm out of here," she kept saying. "I can't stand it another day. I'm losing my mind."

Nova wasn't worried then. She knew they'd end up somewhere else eventually.

When the time came, though, leaving was different. No social worker to transport them. No paperwork for adults to sign. Bridget didn't even glare at the failed foster parents and say goodbye. Nova and Bridget just piled into a car and drove away. This was not their routine, which made Nova's tummy hurt because she hated goodbyes, but she hated deviating from the routine even more.

"Don't worry!" Bridget had kissed Nova's forehead. "I'll take care of you like I've always taken care of you!"

Now Bridget was gone.

And Nova was worried.

She rocked back and forth on her knees, hugging NASA Bear to her chest, and glanced around her newest bedroom. The first room she'd ever had all to herself.

Diagonal from the door was a double bed with a fancy carved headboard. The mattress was soft, the pillow was softer, and the blanket was plush and purple, covered in tiny silver stars.

It was too big.

The bedroom was long but narrow. It had two windows, one facing the front yard and the other facing the back. Out back there was an in-ground pool, covered up for the winter. Out front a pathway leading up to the door was guarded by two giant stone lions. At midnight the town switched off the streetlights, which made Nova happy because total darkness meant she could see the Big Dipper lurking along the horizon, where the sun set shortly before dinner each night.

It was too nice.

The upstairs bathroom had a tub long enough to stretch out in. The kitchen always smelled of fresh-baked brownies or banana bread and the color television had a remote control. Most rooms had wall-to-wall carpeting. There were lots of windows through which the sun shone.

It was too much like a home.

Nova didn't want it to start feeling like home. Bridget always warned, "If it feels like home, it's harder to leave."

Nova hugged her teddy bear tighter, trying to picture her big sister in the bedroom beside her. What had Bridget been thinking, deciding to run away like that? It was already January 1986, and in August she'd be eighteen. Then Bridget could raise Nova herself, like they'd always planned.

Only Bridget was gone.

And Nova was lonely.

"You'll start school on Monday," new foster mother Francine warned during breakfast.

Nova hated new schools more than she hated new foster families. New schools always spent the first week or two testing her and always came to the same conclusions: "Cannot read. Does not speak. Severely mentally retarded."

Bridget hated the word *retarded*.

"My sister's not dumb," she'd tell anyone who'd listen. "She's a thinker, not a talker."

The truth was, Nova rarely spoke and when she did, she had difficulty controlling her volume, so sometimes she'd be whispering on a crowded playground and other times she'd be shouting in church. Even when she did manage to find the right sound, forming a whole word was its own challenge. She could say "Oh" or "Kay" but not "Okay." She could say "Wah" or "Ter" but not "Water." She could say "Coo" or "Kee" but not "Cookie." And sometimes when she'd try to say a simple word like "Cat" an entirely different word would come out, like "Boo," which didn't make sense to anyone, not even Bridget.

Most of the time Nova didn't bother to speak at all.

Rocking back and forth on top of the fluffy blankets in the bedroom she had all to herself, Nova wondered for the two millionth time where Bridget had gone and whether she would keep her promise to return in time to see the first teacher skyrocket into space.

"No matter where we end up," Bridget had said,

"even if we have to be separated for a while, I'll come back to see NASA make history, okay? I wouldn't miss it for the world."

Both sisters had been dying to see *Challenger* launch ever since President Reagan announced the contest to find the perfect teacher over a year ago. Nova was glad the waiting was almost over. She wondered if Bridget was glad too.

Nova kissed NASA Bear's belly. His plastic bubble astronaut helmet pressed against her forehead. He had been a gift from their mama, who had very strange ideas about how the 1969 moon landing actually happened.

"Government orchestrated!" Mama liked to say. "All on a soundstage, babies, thanks to movie magic! Did you see the way the astronaut's boots kicked up dirt? The way the flag waved? There's no wind on the moon, girls! How was it waving? It was government orchestrated, that's how! That means the government made it up, to trick us!"

Their mama thought a lot of things were government orchestrated.

"Nova, honey?" foster mother Francine called through the cracked-open bedroom door. "How about we go to the store and get you some school clothes? You've almost grown out of everything the last family sent."

Most of what the last family had sent wasn't even hers, but they needed it to seem like they'd been providing more than fraying sweaters and too-small stretch pants so they sent along a big cardboard box full of clothes their other foster daughters were growing out of. They kept the heavy winter coat they'd bought for Nova and all the slouch socks Bridget had given her for her twelfth birthday.

The only clothes in the box Nova would willingly wear were three pairs of pj's, one pair of red overalls, and two T-shirts she'd inherited from her sister. The first had the words ONE SMALL STEP on the front with the moon landing date on the back, JULY 20, 1969. The second was from David Bowie's 1978 World Tour, black with red and blue print, which they'd found at a thrift shop.

Nova's other possessions included NASA Bear, Bridget's Walkman and favorite mix tape, the Little People figure who looked like an astronaut, the one they'd stolen from a previous foster home where they had so many Fisher Price sets no one would notice, a small spiral-bound notebook, *The Little Prince* by Antoine de Saint-Exupéry, a few faded photographs, a box of sixty-four Crayola crayons, and a silver-banded mood ring with a sky-blue stone that didn't change color anymore. Francine and Billy had given Nova a toy box—her first-ever toy box—in which she could keep her treasures. It was a large wooden crate with JOANIE ROSE stenciled across the top in flowery Carnation Pink letters.

"It belonged to our daughter when she was little,"

Francine had explained. "Pink is Joanie's favorite color. She's so happy to have you here, Nova. She hated being the youngest and the only girl. Growing up with three big brothers was lonely, I think."

James, Joseph, and John. Those were the three big brothers. Shortly after Nova arrived at the Wests', Billy had pointed to a picture of the boys hanging on the wall above the television. "My three sons!" he'd said proudly. "Doctor James, Carpenter Joseph, and Recreation Director John."

Nova couldn't ask where the three brothers had gone, whether they'd disappeared like Bridget. *Maybe they went to the moon,* thought Nova, picturing the boys from the picture floating weightlessly above a crater. She imagined James with a stethoscope and Joseph with a hammer but didn't know what a recreation director might have.

"Every Christmas Joanie wrote Santa asking for a little sister, but we had our hands full then."

Nova glanced down at Francine's hands. They weren't full anymore. They were placed upon the wooden lid of the toy box. Her nails were long and shiny and she wore three rings, two sparkly gold ones on her left hand to show she was married, and one thin silver band on her right pinkie. Her fingers ran over the letters spelling JOANIE ROSE like there was something in the box much more important than toys.

"When the weather gets nicer," Francine had continued, "we'll buy some wood stain and paint and have it redone with your name."

Nova stared at the toy box and imagined her name in place of Joanie's. NOVA BEA VEZINA. It was a perfect name. Bridget said so, and Bridget never lied.

"Nova?" asked Francine again, poking her head into the bedroom, tugging Nova free from the memory. "Clothes shopping?"

Nova shook her head one-two-three-four times. She did not want to go clothes shopping. She hated trying things on, pants that pushed against her belly and socks that touched her ankles and shirts with itchy tags and dresses—oh, the dresses! Nothing could be worse than something she had to wear tights under. Tights stretched from her waist to her feet and always, *always* had a seam line across her toes. She *hated* lines across her toes.

Francine stepped all the way into the room, which made Nova hug NASA Bear tighter. "Mrs. Steele told me how you feel about clothes, but we need to find at least enough to get you through this first week of school, right? You can't wear jammies forever."

Mrs. Steele had been Bridget and Nova's social worker for most of the years they'd been in foster care. She was okay. Except she used the R-word a lot.

Cannot read. Does not speak. Severely mentally retarded.

Bridget hated the R-word.

"Nova?"

Nova let out an involuntary squeak. That happened sometimes. She couldn't help making noise, even when she was trying her hardest not to.

Francine sat cross-legged at the foot of the bed, facing Nova.

"I'm sorry. I know this must be very difficult. But Billy and I are so happy to have you here. So is Joanie."

Billy was Francine's husband, Nova's new foster father. Joanie was their daughter, home from college on winter break.

"Mm," said Nova, nodding her head ever so slightly. She imagined what Bridget would say: "Suck it up, Super Nova, 'cause you can't go to school nekkid."

Nekkid. Nova's lips curled into a smile, then parted to let out a high screech, followed by several hiccupy squeals. Her body twitched, her hands flailed. Bridget loved the word *nekkid*.

"Are you laughing?" asked Francine, her smiling growing into a grin. "I haven't heard you laugh before! I love your laugh!" Francine laughed too, for some reason, so Nova kept right on flailing and twitching and laughing about Bridget and *nekkid*. She laughed until tears stung her eyes. She used NASA Bear's matted furry leg to wipe them away. *Nekkid. Oh, Bridget!*

"Come with me, Nova. You can pick out whatever's comfortable. If you want to buy nothing but T-shirts and overalls, that's fine. No dresses, I promise."

Francine stood, holding out her hand. Nova mulled

this over for a moment before taking Francine's hand and allowing herself to be led out of the bedroom, not loosening her grip on NASA Bear.

Maybe clothes shopping with Francine wouldn't be *too* bad.

Maybe they could buy slouch socks.

10

JAN 18, 1986

Dear Bridget,

T-minus ten days until *Challenger* launch.

Today is Saturday. I don't know how long it's been since I got here, but you missed Christmas. I missed you on Christmas. It was not Christmas without you.

I'm sorry I did not write before today. My hands and arms and shoulders were hurting and I was tired. Plus maybe I was angry.

I am angry because you are gone.

I am angry because Christmas was not Christmas without you.

I am angry because only you can understand my letters, because everyone else calls them scribbles, because without you here to see the words I try to make, it's like I'm writing to nobody.

I'm ready for you to come back.

I have a new foster family.

The mom is Francine West. She is tall and skinny with light skin and light hair. The dad is Billy West. He

11

is shorter and rounder with dark skin and no hair. They have a daughter named Joanie West who lives here, except when she's at college, plus three grown-up sons who live far away.

Francine says I am their first-ever foster child.

I laughed today and she did not yell "Stop making that weird noise!" like our last foster mother. Francine laughed when I laughed but it did not feel mean like when kids laugh.

Will you be mad, Bridget, if I laugh and you're not here?

Will you be mad if I laugh with Francine?

I know you always say "Foster families are not forever families" and "We should not get attached," but I think you might like Francine. She talks to me the way people talk to you. Not too loud and too slow, the way they talk to me.

She talks like I am a person.

This is a nice house, Bridget. There are four big bedrooms. One is for Billy and Francine, one is for Joanie, one is for me, and they said the downstairs one is for guests. My bedroom has a door in the back of the closet that goes to the attic, which is my favorite part of the house, even though there is a lot of dust that makes me sneeze. The attic is dark with sloped wooden ceilings and a round window at the far end. It is a perfect place to pretend to be in space.

In the upstairs living room, they have cable. Have you seen cable? Cable is where there are extra TV channels and one is called Nickelodeon, special for kids. Nickelodeon has a show of *The Little Prince*. The same one from our book! Joanie puts it on for me every single day and does not get mad when it makes me so happy I jump on the couch and squeak and flap. She just says "Sit quietly, Nova," and then I try to sit quietly.

The launch is in ten days, Bridget. It was in the newspaper this morning. Billy read it out loud: "T-minus ten days until *Challenger* launches!"

I am glad it is ten days. I can count up to ten and I can count down from ten. Ten is my best number! Every countdown starts with ten.

This means you have ten days to find me so we can watch it together like you promised.

Maybe if you decide it's okay to be a foster kid again, Francine and Billy will let you have the guest room.

It does not lead to the attic or even the basement, but it has carpeting.

Please come back.

I miss you.

Love,
Your Super Nova

Chapter Two

Francine held Nova's hand as they walked up the stairs to Jefferson Middle School, a rectangular two-story building with a brick façade and windows that stretched from ceiling to floor on either side of centered double doors. Nova hugged NASA Bear with her free arm. Billy led the way, talking the entire time.

"You'll love it, Nova. All our kids went to Jefferson from fifth grade through eighth. That was back before they moved the fifth graders into the elementary school building to make way for more specials. Do you know about specials?"

Nova made her "Mm" sound, which the Wests were learning to recognize as a yes. Some of her old schools called classes specials if they were taught by teachers who were not the classroom teacher. Other schools called them electives or extras or enrichment courses.

"Here they offer all the regulars—music, art, gym—but they've also got home economics for the girls, and woodshop for the boys, and once a week they have X-Block."

Nova cocked her head to the side.

"I know what you're thinking," said Billy. "What the heck is X-Block?"

Nova smiled. That *was* what she was thinking—minus "the heck."

"X-Block is the most special of the specials. You can sign up for a fun class you want and you get to pick a new one each quarter. They started that when our son John was in sixth grade. It was his idea. He wrote up a formal proposal and presented it to the teachers during a faculty meeting. We were so proud of him . . ."

Billy's voice cracked. Francine picked up where he left off.

". . . for taking the initiative. Johnny was a shy, sweet boy who always wanted to learn new things but had trouble making friends. This helped him meet kids with similar interests."

"Now he's a recreation director," said Billy. "Planning activities for at-risk kids!" He gave Nova's shoulder a squeeze. She pulled away.

Francine continued the explanation.

"During X-Block, kids can decide whether they want to do band, chorus, soccer, softball, archery, book club, dance . . . We talked to Mrs. Pierce; she's going to be your special education teacher, and she said kids who are more—more like you—they usually stay in the special ed room during X-Block, but we thought . . . well . . ."

"We thought you'd prefer something fun!" Billy finished. "They have a planetarium here and offer astronomy this semester, so we requested that for you. Do you know about astronomy? Have you ever been inside a planetarium?"

Nova tapped her right middle finger and her forefinger rapidly against her chin. She hadn't been in a planetarium before, but of course she knew all about astronomy. The study of stars, planets, moons, comets, galaxies . . . Bridget had taught her lots about astronomy.

"Mm," she answered finally, even though the answer was technically half yes, half no.

Francine and Billy smiled. They had reached the double doors. Billy knocked on the glass. From inside the building, a heavyset man wearing a blazer with jeans was making his way toward them. He opened the door.

"If it isn't Mr. and Mrs. West!" The man shook Billy's hand and kissed Francine on the cheek. Nova promptly stuck her hand out like Billy, ready to shake, because there was no way she wanted this man's beard and lips anywhere near her face.

"How polite!" exclaimed the man, taking Nova's hand. "You Must Be Nova!"

"Mm," said Nova. She was certainly using that word an awful lot today.

"My Name Is Principal Dowling!" Like so many of her former teachers and foster parents, Principal Dowling emphasized each word as if Nova couldn't hear well. "Nice To Meet You! Ready For The Grand Tour?" He put his face close to hers so she had to look at him. She did not make her "Mm" sound or look at his eyes, but she did notice his front teeth, which were crooked like her own, before shifting her gaze to the yellow-and-blue-tiled floor.

"We're ready," said Francine. "Lead the way!"

The school was as flat and rectangular on the inside as it was on the outside. From the main entrance, hallways stretched to the left and to the right, and a wide staircase stood before them.

"We had a long talk with the powers that be and determined it would be best for you to go back to sixth grade," explained Billy. Nova narrowed her eyes. She was already halfway through seventh grade. Why go backward? You only went backward when you were counting down to lift-off. Did this mean she would repeat fifth grade next year and fourth the year after that? She pictured herself seventeen like Bridget, squished into a kindergarten desk, and frowned.

"You Will Love Sixth Grade!" Principal Dowling was smiling with too many (crooked) teeth. Nova covered her ears and hummed but she could still hear him talking to her foster parents.

"As you know, upstairs we have seventh grade, eighth grade, and the planetarium, but unfortunately Mr. Mindy keeps it locked up when he's not here, so she'll have to wait and see on Wednesday. That's when sixth grade has X-Block." He turned to Billy. "Did you tell her about X-Block?"

"We sure did!" said Billy, smiling. He nudged her playfully. "Right, Nova?"

"Mm," she said.

It seemed like an okay school. The walls were lined with recently repainted lockers. (Nova knew they were recently repainted because she touched one and got paint on her finger, which she licked off. It did not taste as orange as it looked.) Above the lockers and on teachers' doors were posters and projects by students who'd designed their own book covers. Nova recognized one title right away: *Bridge to Terabithia*. Bridget had read her the first two chapters but ended up finishing it on her own one night while Nova was asleep. She'd apologized in the morning, explaining she "just had to" know the ending. Nova didn't mind. Bridget had promised they'd start *A Wrinkle in Time* next, and Nova already loved it for its dusky blue cover with green and black circles.

"Sad book." Francine tapped the *Bridge to Terabithia* poster. "I don't think kids should read books about other kids dying."

Kids dying.

Nova shuddered.

Kids should not be dying. Bridget had taught her that last spring when she'd done a project on starvation in Ethiopia.

"This shouldn't happen." Bridget slammed her research book shut. "Not to kids. Kids don't deserve to die. Leave the dying for the people who start the wars that create the famines, not the kids who can't do a damn thing about it!"

Nova didn't understand words like *starvation* and *famine* and didn't have the first idea where Ethiopia was (far from their home in New Hampshire, she guessed), but she understood that it was bad, because Bridget swore. And Bridget almost never swore. Not in front of Nova.

"Do you see?" asked Billy, jostling Nova out of the memory. He was pointing at another poster, which featured a girl jumping over a brook. "That's what your classmates are learning."

Nova couldn't understand all of the words on their projects, but she could tell that these kids weren't reading picture books, which were the only ones teachers ever gave her. They usually weren't even good picture books. Each boring book had two or three boring words on each boring page under boring pictures. *See cat. See cat run. Run, cat, run!*

Nova hated those books.

Only Bridget read to her from chapter books and

novels, ones that looked like *Bridge to Terabithia. The Little Prince* had been their favorite since forever, but they'd also shared *Peter Pan, Alice in Wonderland, Harriet the Spy,* and all seven books about spunky Ramona Quimby and her big sister, Beezus.

Nova was still staring at the *Bridge to Terabithia* poster when she began to wiggle. The wiggle grew into a dance. She squeezed her legs together, bouncing on her toes.

"I'll take her to the bathroom!" Francine hurried Nova down the hall. Nova was relieved. She often didn't realize she had to GO until it was almost too late, and even when she did recognize the signs, she didn't know how to tell anyone. At home she could run into the bathroom and screech if she couldn't get her overalls off fast enough by herself, until Francine or Joanie came to help.

Once Nova closed herself into a stall, she was able to look around. The bathroom walls and ceiling were white, but the stall doors were the same orange as the lockers. Some girls had used permanent markers to write their names in block letters, visible even through the new paint job. Nova reached out to trace a bubbled *B* with her fingertip. *B* for *Bridget.*

After she flushed, Nova pulled her overalls up and stepped out of the stall so Francine could fasten them. Francine also reminded Nova to wash her hands with soap (which was silly because Nova *always* washed her hands with soap), then led her back out into the hall.

"We're going to show you the special education room now, Nova. Mrs. Pierce is looking forward to meeting you." Principal Dowling glanced at Billy. He wasn't speaking in that strange forceful way anymore, which made Nova happy.

"Right this way, m'dear," said Billy in a silly English accent. He took Nova's hand and twirled her under his arm. She let out a squeak of laughter.

Principal Dowling unlocked the door to the large, brightly decorated classroom at the end of the hall. "Mrs. Pierce just returned to us in September. I don't know if she mentioned it at your meeting last week, but she spent two years on sabbatical in California, studying the latest techniques for teaching children with autism. We're excited for her to implement what she's learned."

Nova glanced around. Across from her was a massive poster of the solar system that made her breath hitch in her throat. Glossy and bright, featuring all nine planets and Earth's moon. It was beautiful. Too beautiful. Her body began to bounce. Even NASA Bear was excited.

Billy and Francine encouraged her to look around, to see what else the classroom had to offer. It wasn't easy, but she tore her eyes from the solar system.

Along one wall were bookshelves, and taped up all over the other wall were laminated cards featuring shapes and colors, so many shapes and colors. By the bookshelves were posters from nursery rhymes and a small play area with a beanbag chair, plus regular chairs on a bright blue rug arranged in a semicircle. Near the laminated cards were desks and tables, each with a name tag for the student who sat there. Nova closed her eyes and covered her ears as Billy and Francine led her around, prompted by the principal.

Exploring this new classroom reminded Nova of her very first day in her very first school. She was five years old and small and scared. She and Bridget had just moved in with their very first foster family, who said it was "high time" Nova started school. Nova did not want it to be "high time." She hated not knowing what to expect. She hated new and unfamiliar places. And she hated being away from Mama. But Bridget was there. Bridget rode the bus with her. Bridget walked her to her classroom. Bridget held her hand the whole way.

"I am right down the hall if you need me," Bridget promised. "Room two twelve. Can you remember that? Two twelve."

"Mm," said Nova.

"Don't say 'mm,' Nova. Say yes. You can do it. Yes."

"Yeh."

Bridget smiled and kissed Nova's forehead.

"Good job! You are so smart. Don't let them tell you you're not smart. I know you're smart and you know you're smart, but if you only say 'mm' they're gonna think you're not smart. Say 'yes' and 'no.' You can say 'no,' right?"

"Yeh."

"Say it now. 'No.' Your turn."

"No."

"Great job!" Bridget hugged her again. "Kinder-garten will be great. It's all coloring and singing and nap time and stories and playing with blocks. You're good at all of those things, right?"

"Mm."

"Not 'Mm'! *Yes.* Listen, I'm right down the hall in room two twelve. If anyone is mean to you, you come get me and we'll leave, okay? We'll walk right out of this school and never come back. Okay?"

"Kay."

"Okay?"

"Kay-kay."

"*Oh*-kay."

"*Oh-kay.*"

"Good. I'm proud of you. Have fun, Super Nova."

But Nova did not have fun. The teacher started by asking, "What is your name?" Nova did not answer.

"Don't you know your name?" Teacher asked.

Nova did not answer.

"Are you shy?" Teacher asked.

Nova did not answer.

"Hel-lo?" Teacher sang, waving a hand in front of Nova's face. Nova jerked away. The teacher was too close. Nova did not like anybody too close except Bridget. Or sometimes Mama. She screeched and swatted toward Teacher.

"Excuse me, young lady!" Teacher's voice was getting too loud. "You need to answer!"

Nova backed up and flapped her hands in the air, making her squeaking noise. When Teacher reached toward her, she closed her eyes and covered her ears, trying to block out the world.

The kindergarten classroom was very noisy.

Pencil sharpener sharpening.

Marbles spilling out from a metal can onto the floor.

Crayons rolling from a cardboard box onto the table.

Birds chirping outside.

Kids chirping inside.

It was too much.

Nova dropped to her knees and rocked back and forth, squeaking, eyes still closed.

"Get up," said Teacher, tugging at her arm.

"Bidge!" Nova screamed for her big sister to save her. "Bidge, Bidge, Bidge!"

"What are you saying?" Teacher yanked Nova roughly to her feet. "We don't allow curse words in this classroom, young lady. Last chance. Tell me your name or it's straight to the principal's office with you!"

She was holding Nova's arm too hard. Nova could feel skin against her skin and she hated skin on her skin. Where were they going? She hated the not knowing even more than she hated skin on her skin. Frightened, she hit Teacher over and over, wanting her to let go, but Teacher did not.

"Students, sit on the rug," said Teacher. "I will be right back."

She dragged Nova down the hall still screaming and hitting.

"Bidge! Bidge!" Nova could not remember which room her sister was in. She started to cry. She could not move her feet. It was as if she'd forgotten how to walk. Her cloth sneakers were dragging on the carpet. Nova did not know where they were going. Nova did not understand why she was in trouble. Nova wanted Bridget to save her, to bring her home. Not to the foster home, but to Mama's home. Their real home. That was where their rocket ship was.

"Walk!" Teacher yelled.

"Help!" Nova tried to say, but only noises come out, noises that didn't sound anything like "help." She cried harder, so hard she began to cough. She couldn't see through her tears.

Suddenly, Bridget came tearing out of a classroom. Bridget yanked her sister roughly away from the teacher and wrapped her in a tight hug.

"What are you doing?" Bridget shouted. "Don't touch her!"

"Bidge!" cried Nova, but it was even harder to speak

now than before, because she couldn't stop coughing and crying. She hoped Bridget would tell Teacher what she'd been trying to say.

"I'm taking her to the office!" said Teacher, her round face purpling. "She was cursing and hitting me. She wouldn't tell me her name."

"My sister doesn't know how to curse," Bridget said. She used her sleeve to wipe Nova's runny nose. "And she was only hitting you because you scared her!" Then Bridget said a bad word.

"You're both going to the office!" Teacher pulled Nova by her right arm and Bridget by her left. Nova dragged her feet the whole way. Bridget unleashed every curse word she knew at top volume. That was how Nova knew how mad she was.

"Deal with this," ordered Teacher when they reached the principal's office.

Principal was not happy. He called their foster family. Their foster family was not happy.

Bridget and Nova did not live with them for long.

★ ★ ★

"Nova, everything all right?" asked Francine, tapping Nova's shoulder lightly. Nova jumped. She had forgotten that she was in the Jefferson Middle School special education room. She looked at Francine, then at the window by the desk that was going to be hers.

Francine tried to hug her, but Nova pulled away. She did not enjoy hugging. Francine made a sad sound, like a sigh, and Nova wasn't sure why but it made her feel bad, so she handed Francine NASA Bear.

"Na-ah Beah bebba," she said. She meant "NASA Bear makes everything better."

"I don't understand," said Francine, looking pained. "But I love that you're talking! Can you tell me again?"

"Mm," said Nova. She meant no.

Outside, a fat gray squirrel whipped his way up a leafless tree. Nova gasped. What was the squirrel doing out in this cold weather? She crawled on top of the desk to see him better. He seemed to sense her. He stopped on a low, bare branch and stared back at her, tail twitching.

"Guuhhhh," said Nova, slapping her palm against the window. She wanted to ask why he was out in such cold, but the words would not come out. "Guuhhhgggguhh!"

"Get down, please, Nova," coaxed Billy. When she didn't respond, he put his arms around her waist and removed her from the table, which she did not like. She pulled away.

"We don't sit on tables," Francine admonished, friendly but firm. "You know that."

Nova glanced back at the window. The squirrel was gone.

Now she felt sad. She needed NASA Bear. She looked down at her arms, then at the desk. Where was he? She looked at Francine and Billy. *Oh! There!* Francine was still holding him. With a screech, Nova grabbed one of his legs and yanked him roughly away, hugging him to her chest.

"Are you okay?" asked Francine.

"Mm," she answered, but it was not a yes or no sound. She meant "Mine."

"Nova?" asked Billy. He reached for her. She backed away, certain he would hit her for screaming. But she would not let him. Instead, she hit herself, one-two-three-four times in the side of the head with her free palm.

Gently, Francine took her hitting hand and lowered it. She guided Nova's chin with her thumb. Nova let herself make eye contact with Francine for a second. She did not see anger there, but the feeling of looking right at Francine was intense anyway. Nova wanted to say she was sorry, even though she wasn't sure why she should be. It simply seemed like the sort of thing kids said when adults started staring at them.

"It's okay, Nova," said Francine softly. "Everything's okay."

Nova, feeling calmer, glanced around the classroom. Her gaze settled on the list of rules posted by the teacher's desk.

Quiet Voice
Calm Body
Nice Words
Happy Hands

Listening Ears

Respect Property

Help Others

Be Kind

"Is she reading the sign?" asked Principal Dowling. He sounded surprised.

"Just looking," said Francine pleasantly.

But Francine was wrong.

She *was* reading the sign.

She'd read the whole list, every single rule.

For a second, Nova felt excited, so excited she had to happy-flap her hands and squeak. She'd just read that sign all by herself, every single word! Even *property,* and that was a tough one!

"We were told that Nova can't read anything yet," Francine went on. "She doesn't know the alphabet. But we'll work on it!"

The alphabet?

Nova stopped happy-flapping.

The alphabet was the name for the ABCs. Nova knew her ABCs. Bridget taught her the ABCs when she was six!

She felt her face going hot.

Does not speak. Cannot read. Severely mentally retarded.

Her eyes filled with tears. She needed Bridget. Bridget would tell them, "My sister's not dumb. She's a thinker, not a talker."

The tears burned as they fell. Nova was ready to be

All Done with this tour. She bit between her thumb and her forefinger to keep from crying too hard, but Billy took her hand away from her mouth and held it.

"Is she . . . okay?" asked Principal Dowling.

"I think Nova's a little overwhelmed," answered Francine as she fished a tissue from her purse. "Her social worker told us that happens sometimes. She's an anxious girl, especially in new or unfamiliar situations. We've mostly been keeping her home since they placed her with us, to get used to things."

"Which is precisely why we appreciate you letting us come today!" Billy reached out to shake the principal's hand again. "We want her first day to go as smoothly as possible."

"Of course!" Principal Dowling smiled, but at the same time shot Nova a nervous look he hadn't worn before. Francine held the tissue up to Nova's nose and asked her to blow.

"Francine will be dropping her off and picking her up each day," said Billy as Principal Dowling led the way back to the main double doors.

"I can drop her here and still get to my classroom in plenty of time." Francine tucked a stray lock of hair behind Nova's ear. "The elementary school is right down the road."

"Ah, yes," said Principal Dowling. "How is kindergarten? Got a good group this year?"

Francine nodded. "I love them. They always start off so helpless! Babies, practically, unable to read or write or tie their shoes or color inside the lines, but by the time summer vacation rolls around . . ."

Nova wasn't listening anymore. She wasn't crying anymore either. She was humming softly and holding NASA Bear with one hand, tapping her chin with the other, thinking again about the very first time she'd walked down halls like these, back when she was a kindergarten baby.

School would start tomorrow.

She was not ready.

9

JAN 19, 1986

Dear Bridget,

T-minus nine days until *Challenger* launch.

Tomorrow I start my new school.

I saw it today with no other kids in the building.

It seemed okay.

I liked the special education classroom.

When we walked in, the first thing I saw was the poster of the solar system.

I started to bounce and hum and hum and bounce because it was so beautiful. It was big and huge and shiny with all the planets from Mercury to Pluto, surrounded by stars. I could see Saturn's rings and Jupiter's red spot and cloud-dotted Earth and fiery Mars and gassy brown Venus and ice giant Uranus and cool blue Neptune. Neptune looks like the stone in the mood ring you gave me. You know Neptune is my favorite. Here are the reasons:

It is blue and I like blue.

It is cold and I like cold.

It might have rings and I like rings.

It has two moons and I like moons.

Plus it has huge windstorms and I like huge windstorms.

Last September, when Hurricane Gloria hit New England, we watched the news coverage on television until the power went out. We spent two days in the dark and you told me, "Just pretend we're on Neptune, where winds rage at over one thousand miles per hour!" I wonder how long power would be out on Neptune if people lived there.

Only nine more days until space shuttle *Challenger* blasts off through the stratosphere to float among the stars, Bridget. Only nine more days until the First Teacher in Space gets to see all this for real. Real stars, real planets. Only nine more days until she sees the world from outside the world. You know what that means!

T-minus nine days until I see you again.

"We might have to be apart for a little while," you said. "But when *Challenger* launches, I'll be there. No matter what, I'll be there. I promise."

That's what you said.

You promised.

While I was staring at the nine perfect planets, Billy bumped my arm and whispered, "Don't forget to breathe!" which was a good thing because I think I did forget! To make myself breathe I had to cover my ears and close my eyes so I couldn't look at it anymore, but I can still see cool blue Neptune in my head, round and bright and shiny and perfect.

The classroom walls are perfect too, decorated with shapes and colors. I knew most of the colors from our Crayola box but some I never saw before. I also saw triangle and crescent and circle and square and one shaped like a stop sign.

Do you remember when you taught me colors and shapes, before we went to foster care and I got sent to school? You would hold up each Crayola and say things like "Brick Red, for drawing buildings" or "Cadet Blue, more gray than blue." I liked Lemon Yellow best.

Then you would cut my sandwiches special, hold up the pieces, and say, "Tuna triangle has three sides," or "Ham-and-cheese circle, round like a ball." Peanut butter jelly crescents were my favorite.

My desk is really a table, Bridget. It is a silvery color with a name tag that has my whole name on it, Nova Bea Vezina, black writing on a Crayola Maize background with a red apple in the corner. I love my name tag. I love my table. I even get to sit right next to the window and you know I love to look out windows.

There are lots of bookshelves. I didn't get to look at the books yet so I don't know if Beezus and Ramona are there. Above the bookshelves are posters of Mother Goose rhymes like in my elementary school classrooms except these all had sheep, every single one. There was a Baa Baa Black Sheep and a Little Bo Peep sheep and a Mary Had a Little Lamb sheep. You know I hate sheep.

On the drive to Billy and Francine's house, I was thinking about how it used to be when you were at school but me and Mama stayed home and had fun. I only remember a little bit, like how she liked to braid my hair and kiss my forehead and call me Super Nova. We raked leaf piles to jump in. Sometimes we walked to the brook to skip stones. When I got tired, she carried me. We ate lunch on the couch while watching TV. I drank red-purple Kool-Aid. She drank red-purple wine.

After lunch, she turned on the radio.

I would try not to be scared.

I would tell myself, "Bridget will come back soon."

I knew everything would be okay again once you got back.

Sometimes the radio brought good news.

"The value of gold hits a record high! Over two hundred twenty dollars an ounce! That's why we bury it, Super Nova. The dollar keeps falling, but we'll be fine with our gold!"

Sometimes the radio brought bad news.

"The USSR is testing nuclear weapons! They're detonating neutron bombs! This could be it! The beginning of the end! And where's President Carter?"

Sometimes Mama listened to static instead of the news. Those were sheep days. I wish you were there. It would not have seemed so scary if you were there.

"Communism prevailed when Saigon fell! It's only a matter of time before they come for us! Your father knew the truth. That's why he never came back from Vietnam. Missing in action, that's what they said. He can't get back to us. No place is safe. We need shelter! We have to hide!"

That was when she would lead me to the kitchen. Mama would have me crawl under the table, then she'd put the white woolly blanket over the top so it hung down to the floor on all sides. Once our shelter was ready, she would crawl in too. We would wait and wait while nothing happened, with woolly whiteness all around.

"You're safe now," she'd whisper. "You're safe, Nova Bea."

Safe, in the belly of the sheep.

After a long time passed, or maybe just a little, you would get home and take my hand and say "It's time to come out." Mama would come out too, except if she fell asleep. If she fell asleep, you'd put a pillow under her head and drape the white woolly blanket over her body. Then you would make me a snack.

The whole time in the belly of the sheep all Mama could do was hug me and worry. All I could do was wiggle my hands and wait.

Waiting for you was the worst.

It is still the worst.

I am trying to be on my best behavior here, Bridget. I'm trying not to scream or throw things and I will try to do my best job in this new school. If I am on my best behavior, I will get to stay, and that will make it easier for you to find me. Plus, when you come back, you will say, "I'm proud of you." I will do my best job to make you proud.

Living with Mama, my happiest day was when you gave me the notebook with the crayons to keep with me in the belly of the sheep. Remember how you told me to write to you every day? Well, I'm still writing to you every day. Writing to you made me feel better when I was stuck inside the belly of the sheep. Writing to you makes me feel better now. Writing to you makes me feel like I'm not lost in space, floating all alone among the stars.

Are you writing to me?

I think maybe I could read your letters now, Bridget. I only pretended before, but at Jefferson Middle School there was a big long list of rules. One of them said "Happy Hands." Happy Hands! What does that mean? I know happy means smiling but hands cannot smile. Hands are not one of Peter Pan's happy thoughts. I wanted to tell this to Francine but I could not.

That's when I got sad, Bridget. Not just because I don't know how to have Happy Hands, but also because I read that sign. I read it all by myself, and nobody knows. Francine told Principal I do not even know my alphabet, but right now I can hear you in my head singing the whole song, even "Now I know my ABCs, next time won't you sing with me!" I know every single letter. I know a lot of words.

I need you to come back so you can read my letters, Bridget.

I miss you.

Love,
Your Super Nova

Chapter Three

Nova could not sleep. According to the digital alarm clock Billy had placed in her bedroom the night before, she awoke at precisely 3:04 in the morning. After lying in bed staring at the ceiling for fifteen minutes exactly, she got up, slipped on a brand-new pair of electric-blue slouch socks, and glanced toward the window. It was snowing again. Maybe it would snow so much school would be canceled and she wouldn't have to go.

She hoped so.

As silently as possible, Nova opened the door that led to the attic and climbed the narrow wooden stairs. Careful to avoid tripping over cardboard boxes, old toys, and holiday decorations, she made her way to the porthole-like window in the far wall.

She pressed her nose against the glass and watched as her breath formed a wet, clear circle in the frost. With one finger, she scraped a little of the frost off and slipped it into her mouth. Like ice cream without a flavor. She liked it. She scraped some more. She placed it on her tongue. Scrape, scrape, scrape, until the frost was gone.

Outside, it was dark. No streetlights, no porch lights, not even an idling car in a neighbor's driveway. It was perfect for stargazing, if only she had a telescope.

And knew how to use a telescope.

Nova licked a little of the cold dew that was left on the window before finding the moon. As much as she loved stars and their constellations and beautiful cool blue Neptune, her favorite space rock was definitely the moon. She loved staring at it, imagining herself with Buzz Aldrin and Neil Armstrong, taking those first steps on the hard, white surface, planting the American flag.

"One small step for a man, one giant leap for mankind."

She didn't care what Mama believed about government-orchestrated sound stages. Nova knew in her heart that men had walked on the moon and they'd do it again. Bridget said so.

She closed her eyes and pictured herself as if she was hovering above her own head, hiding in the closet with Bridget at their mama's house, pretending to be rocketing off on a mission to the moon when it wasn't safe to be seen.

The first time they went to the moon, Nova was five

and Bridget was ten. They were in the closet at Mama's house. Mama was in the kitchen with the radio on, and a stranger was there. Mama was yelling at the stranger.

"I know what you're trying to do! You're trying to steal my children!"

"I assure you, Mrs. Vezina, we are not interested in stealing your children, we are only concerned with their welfare. We have had reports that—"

"Nova needs me! And I need Bridget. She's the only one who knows what the television secretly broadcasts after the sign-off!"

Bridget and Nova were usually not allowed to be awake late enough to see the television sign off, but sometimes Mama let them stay up and they all watched Johnny Carson on *The Tonight Show* together. When it was almost time for TV to be done for the night, a waving American flag would show on the screen and the national anthem would play. Mama always made them stand and put their hands over their hearts, and Bridget would sing. Mama said that would make their daddy proud, since he was in the army.

After the national anthem was over, the screen would show a jet. The jet would fly around in the sky in black-and-white and a man's voice would read a poem, the same poem, every single night. Nova loved hearing the poem. She especially loved the beginning and the end.

The beginning went—

Oh! I have slipped the surly bonds of earth
And danced the skies on laughter-silvered wings;
Sunward I've climbed, and joined the tumbling
*   mirth*
Of sun-split clouds—and done a hundred
*   things . . .*

And the end was—

I've topped the wind-swept heights with easy grace
Where never lark, or even eagle flew—
And, while with silent lifting mind I've trod
The high untresspassed sanctity of space,
Put out my hand and touched the face of God.

Next sounded a high-pitched shriek that Bridget said meant it was "time to turn off the tube and go to bed," but that was when Mama was happiest, because static was coming next, and static brought secret news, news that made her smile.

The first time Bridget and Nova made it all the way to the moon, Mama was not smiling. She was crying. Bridget and Nova closed themselves in the closet, where their rocket ship was.

"It's okay," said Bridget. She hugged Nova, then slipped NASA Bear into her arms. "We're not here anymore, Nova. We're headed far away. Close your eyes. It's countdown time. Ten . . . nine . . . eight . . ."

"Mrs. Vezina, I need you to calm down, please," said the stranger.

"Seven . . . six . . . five . . . ," said Bridget.

"Why are you doing this!" asked Mama, but her voice was fading farther away with every counted-down number.

"Four . . . three . . . two . . ."

"Let's take a moment," said the stranger.

"One . . ."

"A moment for what?" asked Mama.

"Lift-off," Bridget whispered.

Nova felt her body become weightless as they entered a field of zero gravity. She was glad they had their space helmets to protect them, since there was no air in space. She was not scared, not anymore, because Bridget knew how to fly the spacecraft, and they were heading to the moon.

"We are leaving earth behind, Nova . . . ," said Bridget in a hushed voice. She lit a flashlight and propped it up behind her globe. "Look! There it is, a blue-and-green ball in the distance! You can open your eyes now. Isn't it far out?"

Nova looked. The earth was lit up from behind. Nova grinned. It must be far out, since they had traveled such a long way. They had gone this far before, but never farther. Never all the way to the moon.

Nova kissed NASA Bear's soft plastic helmet.

From behind her back, Bridget produced a large

white balloon. She blew it up, so big it was almost the same size as the globe, tied it off, and placed it in front of Nova.

"Moon!" Nova said, pointing. Bridget beamed.

"That's right, moon!" Bridget picked up her walkie-talkie and held it to her lips. "Ground Control, space shuttle *NovaBridge* here! We are now safely soaring above the earth at approximately three hundred fifty miles beyond sea level, traveling at a speed of twenty thousand miles per hour. Next stop, the moon. Over."

"Please!" pleaded the distant voice of their mother, somewhere back on Earth. "Please don't take my girls!"

"Moon!" Nova hugged NASA Bear.

"Yes, moon. We made it, Nova," Bridget whispered. "We're safe now. We've just landed. The next thing you'll feel is space dust beneath your feet." Then she sang a line from their favorite song, "Space Oddity" by David Bowie, about an astronaut named Major Tom communicating with Ground Control: *"Now it's time to leave the capsule, if you dare!"*

Nova nodded. She could no longer hear anything happening down on Earth.

She could not hear the stranger calling their names.

And she could not feel anything either, not anything except zero gravity and moon rocks.

She did not feel it when Bridget helped her into her jacket or when Mama kissed her on the forehead.

She did not feel it when a police officer gently picked her up and carried her to an unfamiliar car.

And she did not make noise, not even a hum, to drown out the Earth sounds around her.

She did not make noise when the social worker buckled her into the backseat or when Bridget took her hand and held it tight.

She did not make noise when they were driven away from Mama.

She was too far away. On the moon.

With her big sister.

Safe.

★ ★ ★

Alone in the attic Nova was not tired, not at all, not even with her eyes closed, but when she opened them again, light was streaming through the round attic window, the snow had stopped falling, and Francine was calling her from the bottom of the stairs.

"Are you up there, Nova?"

"Ah!" called Nova, scrambling to her feet. How long had she been asleep? Did she miss the first day of school?

She rushed down the stairs to the bedroom, where Francine was waiting.

"Thank goodness! I panicked when I saw your empty bed. Come on, let's get you dressed, then we'll eat

breakfast. Billy's making his special chocolate chip banana pancakes."

Nova could already smell bacon, the scent waft-
ing up through the air vent in the floor. Her tummy
growled. She pictured Billy at the stove, flipping flap-
jacks. He liked to cook, especially unhealthy things his
wife wouldn't make for him. He was supposed to be
watching his weight, she'd said.

"But I have a sweet tooth!" he'd said.

Nova didn't know whether any of her teeth were
sweet too, but she did enjoy the red velvet cupcakes Billy
had let her help frost last weekend.

Francine helped Nova into one of the outfits they'd
picked out on Saturday, a pair of blue denim overalls
with a pocket in front over a long-sleeved midnight-blue
shirt with silver dots that looked like distant stars. Nova
let Francine brush her hair, even though she hated to
have her hair brushed. Francine plaited it in two thick
braids, which she called "just darling." Nova scowled.
She did not want to be darling.

"Remember, they'll bring you to the bathroom before lunch and again at the end of the day, but if you
have to go when it's not time, try to get Mrs. Pierce's
attention, okay? I told her you might need help with the
overalls. A teacher's helper will be with you at all times. I
packed extra clothes in case you have an accident."

Nova's face reddened. She hadn't had an accident in

school in two whole years and didn't plan to have one on the first day at Jefferson Middle either.

"All right, Nova?" asked Francine. She pressed her palm to Nova's forehead. Nova pulled away.

"Pancakes are ready!" Billy called up from the kitchen.

Nova forgot about feeling upset. She hurried down to the kitchen. Joanie was already settled at the table, swirling crispy bacon in Mrs. Butterworth's. Nova took her usual place at the table, suddenly starving.

"I'll tape *The Little Prince* on the VCR for you," said Joanie, smiling. "Would you like that? We can watch it when you get home, 'kay?"

Even though she would like that, Nova did not answer "Kay-kay." She was too nervous to talk.

An hour later, Nova found herself drowning in a sea of students. With everyone else around, the halls of Jefferson Middle School didn't seem so wide and welcoming. Too many competing sounds, too many unfamiliar smells, too many bodies bumping into each other. It was exactly like every other school. She should've known it would be. Francine guided her to the special education classroom at the end of the hall, as planned. Covering her ears while she walked, Nova felt like a dog being led to the back room of a pound. She'd seen *Lady and the Tramp*. She knew how it worked. Bridget had told her. "The pound's back room is where they go to die."

Nova knew the back room was bad because dogs

seemed sad to go there, but she wished she could ask, "What happens *after* they die? Do they come back? Do they get adopted? Why does it make them sad to die in the back room?"

When they arrived, Mrs. Pierce was seated at her desk, writing on a giant calendar.

"You must be Nova!" Mrs. Pierce stood to greet them at the door. "Oh, those braids! Francine, she's just darling!"

Nova scowled, hands still pressed firmly over her ears. There was that word again. *Darling.*

"And who's this?" Mrs. Pierce poked NASA Bear's tummy.

"This is Nova's astronaut teddy," said Francine, handing the bear to Nova.

Nova realized that no one but she and Bridget knew NASA Bear's name, and without Bridget around, it was possible no one else ever would. The thought made her stomach twist painfully into a pretzel.

Sometimes I hate you, Nova thought.

Immediately another feeling took up space in Nova's gut, forcing out the anger. It made her want to say "I'm sorry" for the second time in two days. She hugged NASA Bear, ignoring the tear that dripped down onto his helmet.

"You're interested in space travel, right, Nova?" asked Mrs. Pierce. Nova did not respond, not even with an

"Mm." "We signed you up for astronomy on Wednesdays. We have a volunteer from the high school who's going to take that class with you."

"Wonderful!" exclaimed Francine as she wiped Nova's cheeks with a tissue from her purse. "How'd you work that out?"

"Juniors and seniors get extra credit for tutoring middle schoolers during study halls. One girl wants to pursue a career in special education or astrophysics and happens to love astronomy too. We figured this would be a perfect experience for her, look nice on her college applications . . ."

Nova tuned out as the conversation turned dull. She wandered over toward her desk table. A skinny-armed, big-bellied boy with a round face and spiky hair sat cross-legged under it.

"Hi," he said. Nova looked behind her. No one was there.

"I'm talking at you!" The boy giggled. "You silly. Wanna sit in my cave? There's a bear out there!" He pointed at NASA Bear. "It wants-a eat us!"

Of all the silly nonsense! thought Nova, quoting *Alice in Wonderland*. She wanted to tell the boy, "NASA Bear is a professional payload specialist. A professional payload specialist is not an astronaut, but a scientist or educator. He or she is chosen by NASA to be a member of the space crew with a special job, like doing research or being the First Teacher in Space. A professional payload specialist would *never* try to eat a human, not so long as freeze-dried fruit was readily available." Bridget had taught her all about professional payload specialists. But since Nova could not tell this to the boy, she set NASA Bear down on the floor and climbed under the table.

"My name is Alex. What's your name is?"

Nova opened her mouth but no sound came out.

"Don't be scared," said Alex, smiling. "Is not a real bear, is pretend."

"Alex, Nova, come out from under the desk, please!" called Mrs. Pierce. "It's Morning Circle time."

Alex took Nova's wrist and led her toward the semi-circle of chairs facing the bookshelves. She thought about pulling away, but she kind of liked how his fingers felt like ice. She scooped up NASA Bear with her free hand on the way by.

Six kids were already seated. Three boys, three girls. Behind them sat two adults, one man, one woman. *Very even.* Nova smiled. She liked even because it meant balanced, symmetrical, the same. Mrs. Pierce sat facing them with her back to the books, beside an easel, with a stack of cardboard cutouts on the floor beside her. Mrs. Pierce was a woman, so that made one more girl than boy, but since NASA Bear was a boy Nova supposed it was okay.

"Good morning, class!" Mrs. Pierce said.

"Good morning!" chorused Alex and a few of the

other kids. Nova noticed right away that two of them—one boy, one girl—did not say anything. The boy was bouncing in his chair, making clicking noises with his tongue against his teeth. The girl was sitting in a wheelchair with her head lolled to the side. That looked uncomfortable. Nova reached toward the girl to help her but the lady teacher blocked her hand.

"Class, we have a new student," said Mrs. Pierce. "This is Nova. Nova, can you wave to the kids?"

When Nova did not respond, the lady teacher picked up her hand and waggled it. Nova pulled away.

"Nova is twelve years old and in sixth grade with Mr. O'Reilly. Let's go around the circle and introduce ourselves to Nova. We will say our names, our ages, and one thing we like to do." Mrs. Picrce picked up one of the sheets of cardboard and placed it on the easel. On it, each student's name was listed beside their picture. (Nova's had only a hand-drawn smiley face, no photograph.) Mrs. Pierce tapped the name at the top. "Alex, can you start?"

Alex had chosen the seat closest to Mrs. Pierce. He stood up, arms straight down by his sides, like a soldier.

"My name is Alex. My age is thirteen years. I like basketball."

"Great, Alex," said Mrs. Pierce. "Next?"

The next two were girls who talked: Mallory, who was twelve and liked horses, and Mary-Beth, who whispered "eleven" but did not say what she liked. Then they reached the boy who was bouncing. The guy teacher called him Buddy, age eleven. When Buddy waved at Nova, he turned his hand the wrong way, so he was really waving at himself, but the guy teacher said "Good job" anyway and handed him a piece of candy. Nova copied him, waving the wrong way, but no one gave her candy.

Luke and Thomas were next. Both boys, both thirteen. Luke had a wispy mustache forming on his upper lip, while Thomas sounded like he had a stuffy nose. Nova didn't listen to what they liked because she was too worried about having to remember all these names. *Mrs. Pierce. Alex. Mr. O'Reilly. Mallory. Mary-Beth. Luke. Thomas. Guy teacher. Lady teacher. NASA Bear.* Nova immediately began assigning them nicknames to help her remember: *Bouncing Buddy. Quiet Mary-Beth. Wispy Lip Luke . . .*

"Last but not least, this is Margot." Mrs. Pierce patted the knee of the girl in the wheelchair, then tapped her name on the list. "Margot loves music, especially Madonna. Right, Margot?"

Music Margot didn't respond. Her head was still sort of slumped over. Again Nova reached out to fix her. Again the lady teacher moved her hand away.

"Our helper teachers are Mr. Malone and Miss Chambers. You'll get to know them better this week," said Mrs. Pierce. Nova scowled. *More people with names. More people to know.*

The only person who mattered was Bridget.

"Bidge," Nova whispered, surprising herself. She hadn't tried to say her sister's name in what felt like forever. She closed her eyes and hugged NASA Bear close. NASA Bear, whose name nobody would ever know.

"Nova likes astronauts and outer space," said Mrs. Pierce. "Okay, class! Let's stand for the Pledge of Allegiance."

The rest of the morning went the way school mornings usually did. They stood for the Pledge (Music Margot did not stand), followed by a moment of silence (Bouncing Buddy was not silent), and then Mrs. Pierce read a babyish story (*Where the Wild Things Are* by Maurice Sendak), Alex marked the day on a giant calendar (Monday), Mallory announced the weather (cloudy). Finally everyone went to their desks to work.

"I'll be testing you this week." Mrs. Pierce settled herself beside Nova at the table by the window. "So we can figure out what you know."

Nova sighed.

Another day, another school.

Another week of testing.

8

JAN 20, 1986

Dear Bridget,

T-minus eight days until *Challenger* launch.

It is recess on my first day at Jefferson Middle School. We finished lunch a few minutes ago.

I had a peanut butter and fluff sandwich. Francine made it this morning. She put it in a Crayola Carnation Pink plastic lunch box with My Little Pony from TV on the front. I have a new backpack too. It is also pink. Salmon Pink, not Carnation Pink. You know I hate pink, all shades, but I can't help liking it a little bit now because the backpack is only mine and the lunch box is only mine and I like having things that are only mine, even if they have to be pink.

Fluff tastes funny. Have you had fluff? It is marshmallows but spread out, like butter, which is confusing for my tongue but mostly okay.

This afternoon I will go to the regular sixth-grade class with Miss Chambers and Mallory and Mary-Beth. Mallory likes horses and Mary-Beth talks too quiet.

While we are in social studies, Basketball Alex, Wispy

Lip Luke, and Stuffy Nose Thomas go with Mr. Malone to seventh grade.

Music Margot and Bouncing Buddy stay here with Mrs. Pierce.

That is what Mrs. Pierce said when we made my picture schedule. Except she does not know the special names I gave them.

After Morning Circle, this morning was like other new-school mornings. Testing, testing, testing. Boring, boring, boring. I wish I was at Billy and Francine's house with NASA Bear and my attic window, listening to "Space Oddity," soaring through the stars instead.

Mrs. Pierce set out blue plastic shapes and asked me to touch them.

"Touch triangle. Touch circle."

When I did it right, she gave me a cut-up piece of gummy worm like Bouncing Buddy got for waving backward. I have never gotten candy from a teacher for doing a good job before. When I picked the wrong shape she took my hand and placed it on the right shape. It made me mad to get so many wrong but I could not listen to her asking each shape because there was too much going on, same as in kindergarten and first grade and second and third and fourth and fifth and sixth and the half of seventh I already did before I had to go backward.

There is too much going on, always. Every school, every grade, every classroom, the same.

But not the good kind of same.

Outside there are squirrels even though it is winter.

Inside other kids are noisy.

Plus the ceiling lights have a hum.

And heat rattles through a metal vent.

And pencils scratch papers, which bothers my ears.

And my brain keeps going to the moon. I think I'm full of space dust.

So sometimes when she said "triangle" I thought maybe she wanted "square" because I could not hear "triangle" over all the square sounds around the room.

Then she did the same thing with colors so I started not listening. I think I touched the plastic colors but I do not know if I was looking because in my mind I was seeing outer space and stars and feeling the moon rocks kicking up beneath my feet. So many moon rocks.

I started thinking about the day NASA picked the winner of the First Teacher in Space contest.

July 19, 1985.

You said announcing the winner on my twelfth birthday was fate. You hoped the launch would be scheduled for the day you turn eighteen, which would also be fate. I did not know what fate meant then and I don't know what it means now, but since NASA picked January 1986 instead of August 1986 I guess fate is not something they care about.

Know what I remember best?

When you held up the newspaper and read "Out of more than eleven thousand teachers, NASA has chosen Christa McAuliffe of New Hampshire . . . ," then started screaming, the butterflies already in my tummy fluttered all the way up into my chest. I had to cover my mouth because I thought they might escape! All those teachers, more than I can count, maybe more than there are stars in the sky, and NASA picked one from our New Hampshire! I don't know why I cried. Maybe because of the butterflies, maybe because of the fate, or maybe because your happy-screaming was too loud.

Then you said we were going to rocket out of foster care together just like how the astronauts would be rocketing out of Earth's atmosphere, remember?

That was my favorite part.

That's why you need to come back soon.

I do not want you to miss it.

Recess is over. Mrs. Pierce wants me to put my scribbles away. That's what she called my letters notebook—scribbles. My words to you look like scribbles to her, which makes her just like every other teacher, ever.

Teachers think I cannot read like how Francine thinks I cannot read but maybe they are the ones who cannot read. You could always read my letters. You never called them scribbles. Babies scribble. I'm not a baby.

I miss you.

Love,
Your Super Nova

Chapter Four

Tuesday morning was the same as Monday morning. Mrs. Pierce tested Nova's ability to match objects and pictures by handing her random items from a box labeled MATCH and saying "Match."

Plastic fork. Bubbles bottle. Rubber ball.

Piece of gummy worm. Piece of gummy worm. Piece of gummy worm.

The candy was the right mix of sweet and sour, so Nova tried her best to ignore the squirrels, lights, heat, and other kids so she could concentrate and earn more pieces.

At lunch, Mallory and Alex sat on either side of Nova and talked. They talked a lot. Sometimes they talked at the same time, which made Nova slightly dizzy, so she tuned them both out, but they didn't seem to notice.

At recess, Alex took Nova's hand and dragged her

toward the Morning Circle carpet in front of the book-shelves. Mallory was leading Bouncing Buddy over too, and Quiet Mary-Beth followed a minute later.

"Sit down, Buddy," said Mallory, tugging his hand. She was already cross-legged on the floor. When he sat beside her, she hugged him and he grinned. Unlike Nova, he seemed to love hugs. "We are playing the Ball Game."

"The Ball Game?" whispered Mary-Beth, who both had a lisp and talked so softly Mrs. Pierce was constantly asking her to repeat herself using "a loud and proud voice."

"Yes," said Mallory.

"I don't want the Ball Game," said Mary-Beth so softly Nova almost wasn't sure she'd said anything at all.

"Oh, well." Mallory shrugged. "I'm in charge and I say we're playing the Ball Game." She grabbed a large neon-green bouncy ball from the bottom shelf, the one that held board games and toys instead of books. Nova sat NASA Bear in her lap and crossed her legs like everyone else.

"Mallory can be real bothy," Mary-Beth whispered in Nova's ear.

Nova was pretty sure Mary-Beth meant "bossy," which made her smile. Kids used to call Bridget bossy too, because Bridget always chose and led every game they played, no matter who they were playing with. Nova didn't mind bossy.

"Love-a Ball Game!" said Alex, clapping. "I tell how-a play!"

Everyone except Nova already knew how, but Alex said he wouldn't start explaining until they all put their listening ears on. Finally everyone was quiet, even Buddy.

"You bounce-a ball front-a you five times an' say a color or number or letter or aminal—I mean, animal—then pass-a other kid, who do it too, then if-a other kid forget for five, start again!"

Nova didn't get it. Mallory could tell.

"So I say 'bird,' then I roll it to Alex and he says 'dog,' then he rolls it to Mary-Beth and she says 'pig,' and we keep going until someone gets to five bounces before thinking of an animal. Then the next person picks a category and keeps it going. You know categories, right?"

Nova did not have an answer, but that was fine because Mallory didn't wait for one.

"Think fast! I'll start." Bossy Mallory bounced the ball in front of her four times.

"I never think fatht!" lamented Quiet Mary-Beth.

Nova frowned. She had no idea how she and Bouncing Buddy would play without words.

"Horse!" said Mallory. She rolled the ball to Buddy, who bounced it with one hand and with the other did what looked like the okay sign beside his cheek, slowly moving it away from his face.

"He's signing 'cat,'" explained Mallory as Buddy rolled to Alex. "Good job, Buddy!"

Alex bounced the ball five times. On his fifth bounce, he hollered, "Pigeon!" He rolled the ball to Mary-Beth. She whispered, "Duck," on the fifth bounce. She rolled it to Nova. Nova was bouncing slowly, wondering how she would manage, when her eye caught the nursery rhymes posted on the walls above the shelves. Every single poster had one thing in common:

"Seep!" shouted Nova, louder than she meant to. She pointed at the rhymes.

"Sheep!" repeated Mallory. "Good one! Pass it."

Nova passed to Alex, who yelled, "Hippo!"

It didn't make it back to Nova before the bell rang but that was okay.

This was the first time she had talked to other kids without Bridget, without a teacher, and without quite having the words.

This was the first time she had really, truly felt like part of the group, just like everybody else.

It felt weird.

It felt great.

It felt like being on a roller coaster, not the tick-tick-tick going up, but that first swoosh going down. It felt like fluff on a sandwich, confusing but sweet. And it felt like a soft landing on the moon, right in the Sea of Tranquility, surrounded by other astronauts, guided by Bridget.

The afternoon was not so great, though. More testing.

Nova was sick of gummy worms. Her tummy started to hurt, which reminded her of the day one of their first foster families took her and Bridget to an amusement park, where they rode roller coasters and spinning teacups and ate cotton candy and hot dogs until they felt like throwing up.

Nova closed her eyes and covered her ears, wanting to remember that day, wanting to escape testing with Mrs. Pierce. Wanting to be back with her sister.

★ ★ ★

It was the very end of August right before school would start again. Nova was seven and Bridget was twelve. They had each worn their favorite outfits. Bridget's was a blue-and-green-striped sleeveless shirt with Carnation Pink shorts. Nova's was red OshKosh B'gosh corduroy overalls over a Lemon Yellow T-shirt. They wore matching cloth sneakers with no socks. Nova hated socks then, before slouch socks, because they always had a line across her toes.

At dinnertime, their foster mom was not feeling well. She said she had to throw up, even though she had not been on a single roller coaster or had any cotton candy. Their foster dad took her to find a bathroom. Nova and Bridget sat and waited for them at a picnic table, eating hot dogs and fries.

"Listen, Nova," said Bridget. "I know I've been telling you since they took us away that it's only you and me, right, but these two? They're cool. I overheard them talking to that social worker about what's gonna happen to us next. They sounded real worried we'd end up separated. They don't want that to happen. So I was thinking, maybe they're gonna ask to adopt us? They said we have something important to talk about, right? I think they want to be our forever family. Remember that girl at the last home who kept talking about wanting a forever family? And I told her that was stupid because there's no such thing? Well, maybe I was wrong, okay?"

Nova almost dropped her hot dog. Bridget was never wrong. About anything. Ever.

"If that's what they tell us tonight, if they say they want to adopt us, I'm gonna say it's okay. Okay? But only if you want me to. 'Cause I'll be a teenager next year but you're gonna have more than ten years with these people, right? So it's only okay if you say it's okay. Think it over. Is it okay?"

Nova swirled a fry in ketchup. She thought it over.

"Kay-kay," she said finally. Bridget squealed and hugged her, which made her drop the fry, leaving a grease-and-ketchup mess on her overalls. Bridget cleaned it up.

The foster mom and foster dad came back. It was time to go.

In the car on the way home, they did not tell Bridget and Nova they wanted to adopt them.

They told them they were having a baby.

They told them it would be too much work, having three kids.

They told them a new social worker would be coming the next day: Mrs. Steele.

They told them they'd be moving someplace else.

They told them they were sorry.

That night, before bed, Bridget cried. Bridget never cried. This made Nova's tummy hurt too.

"I was right," Bridget said as she tucked Nova into bed in the room they shared. "There's no such thing as a forever family, Nova. You and me, that's it! We're our own forever family. No one else. You got that? No one else. I'll always take care of you the way I've always taken care of you, just us. You and me and NASA Bear, our space shuttle, and the moon. Okay? Okay."

⋆ ⋆ ⋆

"Nova?" It was Mrs. Pierce's voice, not Bridget's, interrupting her memory. "Nova? Is there something wrong, dear?"

Nova put her forehead down on the desk table, ignoring Mrs. Pierce.

Yes, Nova wanted to answer. *Yes, there is something wrong. Bridget isn't here. That's what's wrong.*

By the time she was ready to work again, the school day was over.

At bedtime, Billy and Francine tucked her in together. Usually they took turns, so this was different, but Nova didn't mind the change in routine too much.

"Mrs. Pierce said you had a hard time concentrating on testing today," said Francine as she drew the blankets up to Nova's chin, the way she liked them. "It's very, *very* important for her to figure out what you know so she can decide what you need to learn. That's why we want you to do your best job, okay?"

"Kay," echoed Nova, annoyed by this. Her best job never seemed to be good enough, so why even try?

"How about *Horton Hears a Who!*?" asked Billy, sliding the picture book from the shelf. Nova hit herself in the temple one-two-three-four times and grunted. Billy and Francine read Dr. Seuss every night. She was as sick of Dr. Seuss as she was of gummy bears.

She reached into the nightstand beside her bed and pulled out Bridget's beloved, beat-up copy of *The Little Prince*. She handed it to Francine.

"Ah."

"You want us to read this?" asked Billy, returning Horton to his place between the Grinch and the Lorax. "I'm not familiar with it."

"It's French," said Francine. "Not this version, this is in English, but the story was originally written in French."

"Ah! Mm!" Nova waved NASA Bear's paw. He wanted Bridget's book too.

The off-white cover of *The Little Prince* depicted a boy with wide-legged, mint-green pants, a red bow tie, and a shock of hair the yellow color of the sun and stars, standing on top of a planet that Nova knew to be Asteroid B-612. On the first page was another color illustration, this one featuring a snake about to make a wild beast his dinner. But Nova's favorite picture from the entire book was on the next page—an elephant inside the body of a boa constrictor. The elephant had been swallowed whole. His one visible eye was rolled up toward the sky as if he was thinking, *Oh, great. I've been eaten.*

"'Grown-ups never understand anything by themselves,'" read Francine, "'and it is tiresome for children to be always and forever explaining things to them.'"

Nova grinned. That was one of Bridget's favorite lines, and hers too.

On page six, the Little Prince insisted the author draw him a sheep. Nova sat up and reached for the book. Bridget always skipped this part because Nova did not care for sheep, all woolly and white, like the blanket Mama used to throw over the kitchen table to keep them safe. She flipped ahead to page nine and gave the book back to Francine.

The Little Prince was very long, as far as bedtime stories go, so they did not make it to Nova's second-favorite part, when the Little Prince meets the Fox. The Fox tells the Little Prince a big secret, the secret Bridget used to whisper to Nova before they'd go to bed at night—"It is only with the heart that one can see rightly; what is essential is invisible to the eye."

"That means we understand each other because our hearts are connected," Bridget would whisper. "Others can't understand us because they know only what they see."

Nova shut her eyes, head back against the soft pillow, and imagined her sister lying there beside her in the bed. She pictured a tiny wooden bridge spanning the length between them, from Bridget's heart to hers, looking just like the one on the *Bridge to Terabithia* cover hanging in the middle school hallway, the one made by a sixth-grade student.

A bridge. Bringing them back together at last.

Francine closed the book and kissed her forehead. Billy said good night.

Eventually, Nova fell into a dreamless sleep.

7

JAN 21, 1986

Dear Bridget,

T-minus seven days left until *Challenger* launch.

Seven days is one week.

That means, in one week, you will come back to watch the launch with me, like you promised. Remember how you promised?

And you never break a promise.

There was another story about it in the newspaper today. Joanie read it to me over breakfast.

"'It's such a quantum leap from what my life has been like,' said McAuliffe." Joanie laughed. "I'll say! One day, you're a high school social studies teacher in New Hampshire, the next you're pretty much an astronaut. I can't even wrap my brain around flying in a plane, never mind a space shuttle. Can you imagine, Nova?"

I said "Mm" because of course I can. I wanted to tell her, "I have imagined it with Bridget for almost my whole life," but since I could not say that I just made NASA Bear raise his paw and nod so Joanie knew he could imagine it too.

Today I played a game with the other kids in my class. It was not an imagination game or a game about space, like what we always played with other foster kids.

It was called the Ball Game.

I had to bounce a ball five times and name an animal. This is the part you will not believe:

I named sheep.

I have never been happy to think of sheep before. I never thought I could be happy to think about sheep but today sheep was my best animal. Like Joanie says, "Can you imagine?"

I want you to meet Joanie. I think you will like her.

She is like you in some ways. She does the stuff you used to do that made our last foster parents mad, like listening to loud music and reading magazines, wearing purple lipstick, and leaving after dinner to "hang out" with friends, but Billy and Francine don't yell "Get back here, young lady!" They just say "Have fun, honey."

Tonight she did not go out. Tonight, her friends came over.

Joanie said they were having a Game Night, but they did not play the Ball Game. They played a boring game with a big rectangle board that had rooms painted on it, like Kitchen and Conservatory, with six little colored wooden pieces that were supposed to be people and teeny tiny objects like a candlestick and a rope.

I did not play the game but Joanie let me stay in her room to watch and eat snacks. She called me "one of the girls." It made me happy but also sad. It made me happy because I liked being one of the girls. It made me feel sad because it made me think of that movie we went to with your friends in December, I think it was called *Clue*. They had a candlestick and a rope in that movie too, just like in Joanie's game.

You and your friends thought the *Clue* movie was funny. You laughed and laughed until you had tears on your cheeks. But I did not laugh at all, not even once, because I thought it was loud and dark and scary and confusing. I wanted to hold your hand but you were already holding hands with that boy who drove us. You said you couldn't hold both of our hands and eat popcorn at the same time. I was mad because you picked his hand over my hand even though he was just your ugly old friend and I am your Super Nova. That's why I knocked the popcorn on the floor.

Then one of your other friends said she could hold my hand instead, but I did not like her skin on my skin. That's why I screamed and hit myself one-two-three-four times. I think you got mad because you dragged me out to the lobby the way Kindergarten Teacher dragged me to Principal's Office. You said, "Please don't ruin this for me, Nova! You have to stop screaming and crying so we can go back in!"

I'm sorry I kept screaming and crying and would not go back in.

I think that maybe means I ruined it for you.

I promise when you come back, we can go to the movies every single day with all your friends if you want, even that boy. I promise I won't ruin it. I'll be one of the girls.

I promise I won't try to hold your hand. And after, maybe we can teach your friends the Ball Game.

I miss you.

Love,
Your Super Nova

Chapter Five

On Wednesday, day three at Jefferson Middle School, Nova woke up excited, got dressed excited, and ate breakfast excited.

It was Planetarium Day.

"Tell her about it, Joanie," Billy said, sneaking a spoonful of sugar into his coffee while Francine wasn't looking.

"You sit back in your chair and look up. The ceiling is curved like you're inside a snow globe. Once the show starts, you feel like you're *there*. I promise, you'll love it."

Nova could not wait to love it.

* * *

"Concentrate, please." Mrs. Pierce put her hand over Nova's hand, which was tapping the picture for PLAN-ETARIUM on her schedule. "We need to finish today's testing. If you can't pay attention on X-Block days, you'll have to miss out on X-Block."

Nova gasped and removed her fingertips from the picture of planets. She tried to concentrate. She did not want to miss out on X-Block, so even though it was hard, she did her best job during testing, like Francine wanted.

"This has been your most productive session yet!" Mrs. Pierce exclaimed when it was time to turn Nova over to Miss Chambers. "I'm proud of you."

Miss Chambers was going to work with Nova on eye contact. She'd call her name, wait for her to look, say "Good looking," and give her a gummy. This was one of Nova's most difficult tasks. She hated looking straight into Miss Chambers's eyes. Anybody's eyes, really. Didn't matter who. She never even liked looking into Bridget's eyes. Nova squinted. Come to think of it, she could not remember what Bridget's eyes looked like. They were brown, right? Like Nova's?

Nova touched her eyelids as if her fingers could figure out the answer.

"Hands down," said Miss Chambers. "Nova?"

Nova did not look at her.

"Nova?" Miss Chambers guided her by the chin until they were staring face to face. "Good looking!"

After lunch, she let herself be led into a game of Hot Potato with Basketball Alex, Quiet Mary-Beth, and

Bouncing Buddy. Miss Chambers tried to get Mallory to play too, but she said, "Why should I? It's a stupid boring baby game for stupid boring babies."

"That is not appropriate!" Miss Chambers scolded. "Apologize to your friends."

"Sorry," said Mallory, but then she looked at Nova and rolled her eyes. Nova tried to roll her eyes back, but without a mirror she wasn't sure if she did it right. She might have just raised her eyebrows.

Miss Chambers held Nova's hands to help her catch and pass the lumpy brown cloth potato before the music stopped. *Mallory is right,* thought Nova. *This is a stupid boring baby game.*

Afternoon time in Mr. O'Reilly's room seemed to last much longer than usual. Nova found herself glancing over and over again at the clock, even though it was the round kind she didn't know how to read.

Finally, X-Block!

Nova's high school student volunteer, Stephanie, arrived. She introduced herself as "a space and science superfan."

"Say hello," prompted Mrs. Pierce. Nova waved.

"We're going to have so much fun! Is your name really Nova? Like, as in supernova? That's so cool. Do you know what that is? A supernova?"

Nova looked at Stephanie (not in the eyes) and shrugged.

"Oh my stars, let me tell you. A supernova is the coolest thing ever!" Stephanie tugged Nova's hand, ready to head to X-Block, but Mrs. Pierce stopped her.

"There are a couple of things we have to go over first," she said. "Wait just a minute, please, Nova."

While Nova waited just a minute, she tapped her fingers against her chin. She knew what a supernova was. *She* was a Super Nova. Bridget said so. She'd said so on the very first night they were in foster care.

And Bridget was never wrong.

★ ★ ★

The very first night Nova and Bridget spent in foster care, they were worried.

Five-year-old Nova was worried about who would take care of them without Mama.

Ten-year-old Bridget was worried about who would take care of Mama without them.

Bridget asked lots of questions but no one answered. Nova had lots of questions but could not ask.

After the sun went down but long before Johnny Carson, their new foster mother settled them into a small bedroom with two beds, no night-light, and silence.

Nova did not want two beds. She was used to sleeping in the same bed as Bridget. Plus she hated being stuck in the dark, like in the belly of the sheep. At Mama's house they had a night-light, plus the light from the hall came in through the open door.

And there was no music. At Mama's house the radio played soft music, Bruce and Bowie and the Top 40 Hits, even when the TV aired static. At the foster home, all they could hear were outside sounds like crickets and trees. With everything in the house silent, every car passing by on the dirt road sounded like a speeding train. It was too much of the wrong kind of noise.

After their new foster mother left the room, Bridget counted out loud to a hundred. Then she got up, turned the light back on, and slipped into bed with Nova.

"I wished on three stars from the bathroom window tonight," Bridget whispered. "Three wishes to go back home to Mama."

Nova did not answer. She just covered her face. She was too upset to think about wishing.

"Nova, it's going to be okay. I'm still here."

Nova did not answer. She just sniffled. She was happy with Bridget, but she wanted Mama too.

"Super Nova?" Bridget nudged her. "Did I ever tell you about the day you were born?"

Nova did not answer. She hugged NASA Bear, snuggled closer to Bridget, and closed her eyes.

"You were born on July nineteenth, 1973," Bridget whispered. "It was the hottest day of the whole year. Mama had the radio on all morning, dancing while we waited for you. She said dancing would help you come faster. When it was time, we grabbed the bag for the hospital, and she asked me to take the radio too, the one with batteries. She didn't listen to static then. She only listened to music. Mama loved music, like me."

Nova smiled. Bridget loved music and she loved to sing. Nova loved listening to her sing.

"It was just us, me and Mama, until you came. Daddy was already gone. He got sent to Vietnam before Christmas to fight some guy named Charlie, but he promised to be back before you were born. He promised and we believed him so we waited and waited."

Nova kissed NASA Bear's helmet. She'd never met her daddy. They were still waiting.

"First the army said he was missing. Later they said he was KIA. That means Killed in Action. Then Mama said sometimes people make promises they can't keep and she cried. She cried a lot, for days and days. But that's another story. On the day you were born, we still thought Daddy was coming back."

Nova had only one picture of Daddy, standing beside a flag. He looked like Bridget if Bridget was a grown-up man in an army uniform. They had the same round face, the same broad shoulders, and the same crooked smile. Nova looked more like Mama. Small nose, delicate hands, frazzled hair. That was all Nova really remembered about how Mama looked, and the only picture she had left of Mama didn't show her face.

"When I first saw you, you looked all red and angry and wailing. I asked Mama what was wrong and she said maybe you were more comfortable in her tummy than in her arms, but she was laughing about it. I wasn't laughing. You hurt my ears!"

Nova smiled. She liked picturing Bridget with her hands over her ears. She knew how it felt to have hurt ears.

"She also said when you were born your face was blue, so red was an improvement. I asked what your name was. She said she didn't pick one yet."

"Oh-ah," said Nova, tapping her chest under the covers.

"That's right," said Bridget. "Nova. Good job saying it."

Nova smiled. She liked hearing "good job" for saying her name. Those *N* and *V* sounds were hard!

"Then two days went by, it was almost time to go back home, and you *still* didn't have a name. Mama and me were sitting in her hospital bed together listening to the radio, watching you sleep. You were a lot cuter sleeping than you were screaming. Bruce Springsteen was on, a song called 'It's Hard to Be a Saint in the City.' Mama loves Bruce like we love David Bowie. The beginning goes, 'I was born blue and weathered but I burst just like a supernova.' The 'born blue' part reminded me of you, so when Mama asked, 'Well, Bridgey-bug, what should we name her?' I said, 'Supernova.'"

Nova smiled. She liked thinking about space and David Bowie and Bruce Springsteen and Mama listening to music.

"Mama thought Supernova was silly. She asked, 'How do we know how super she'll be?' She was only joking but I said, 'Okay, regular Nova, then.' Mama liked it, especially since it came from Bruce, so that's your name and it's perfect. You *are* super. Nothing can hurt you, or bring you down, and no one can take you away from me. You're my Super Nova."

Nova rested her head on Bridget's chest, listening to her heartbeat. She didn't feel so scared once she found out she was super.

* * *

Finally, Mrs. Pierce was through talking with Stephanie, and she and Nova were on their way down the hall. While they walked, Stephanie talked.

"A supernova is the biggest, most massive kind of explosion that exists in the whole galaxy. Maybe in the whole universe. When a supernova happens, a star gets so bright it can outshine all the other stars around it, even brighter than our sun! It's like a gigantic firework in a sea of stars. It explodes because there's a change in its core—that's the center—and . . ." Stephanie glanced up at the clock above the doors that led out to the parking lot. "Oh my stars! We're going to be late! Let's go!"

Stephanie hurried her up the stairs to the planetarium, where the rest of the class was filing in. Stephanie and Nova sat a little apart from everyone else, near the exit.

"Mrs. Pierce said we should in case we need to leave early," Stephanie explained.

As much as Nova hated it when people talked to her too slow and too loud, she wished Stephanie wouldn't zip through everything so quickly and so quietly. While the rest of the class got settled, Stephanie hurriedly hissed odd tidbits of information about astronomy she remembered from her days in middle school. All those whispered words made Nova feel light-headed. She stared straight up at the domed ceiling. Without warning, the lights switched off. Nova jumped in her seat, letting out a squeak and dropping NASA Bear. A couple of kids giggled. Stephanie picked up the bear and handed it back to her.

Their teacher stood in the center of the room. He was so short and skinny he could pass for a fifth grader if not for his long graying beard. He reminded Nova of the garden gnome one former foster family kept in their front yard. Nova pictured him wearing a red pointy hat.

"Greetings, Earthlings! We have two new students in astronomy starting this week. Welcome to the stratosphere, Zach Zbornak and Nova Vezina! Wave to the class!"

Zach Zbornak stood up, held up both hands while

flashing the peace sign, then took a deep bow, which made some of the boys laugh. At Stephanie's urging, Nova stood up too, waved one hand awkwardly (but not backward like Buddy), and sat back down.

"Nice to have you both with us! I'm Mr. Mindy. Let's get started."

Mr. Mindy switched on a lamp in the center of the planetarium and proceeded to lecture in semidarkness about Ursa Major, Ursa Minor, and the reading kids were supposed to have done since last week's class. Nova covered her ears to block out the sound of pencils flying across paper all around her. She felt like she'd fallen into the center of a scratching post surrounded by a dozen angry cats.

Finally, Mr. Mindy clicked the lamp off, hit another switch, and said, "Now we turn to the stars."

Nova's breath caught in her throat. She needed Billy beside her to remind her to breathe. Above her and all around, tiny flecks of light danced and shone. They began as distant pinpricks but grew larger and brighter and closer and closer until they were flying at her face. She reached a hand up, clasping it in midair, certain she could catch one before it slammed directly into her nose. She and NASA Bear were soaring through space as stars whizzed faster than the speed of light, until, abruptly, the movement ceased. Nova braced herself, holding on to the arms of her chair, breathing heavy.

Perhaps they were about to make a soft landing on the moon.

Nova had never felt this way before. It was as if all of the space inside her was filling filling filling and expanding expanding expanding. She wondered if this was how the universe felt in the milliseconds before its creation, when all that there was became hotter and hotter until BANG—an explosion forced the stars and moons and planets and galaxies into formation and set the universe off on a course toward eventual life. This was how Bridget had described the "Big Bang."

"When all that existed up until that point was so dense and thick and full-to-bursting, when it could either collapse in to form a star or explode, it exploded, expanding outward to create everything. Except that it wasn't an explosion, not really, it was more like . . . like a moment in time that created everything. Oh, I'm not describing it well!"

Nova had scrunched up her face, trying to understand, trying to imagine it. As if Bridget read her mind, she exclaimed, "You *can't* imagine it, Nova! That split second billions of years ago resulted in everything existing all of a sudden, born from nothingness!"

Maybe Nova could not imagine or understand it, but here, in the planetarium, she could *feel* it. She knew at any moment she would either collapse in on herself too, or explode. Though she tried to choke it back, a sob escaped her throat. Tears welled up in her eyes as the stars illuminated in the dome surrounded and consumed her. It was beautiful, much more beautiful than the solar system poster or the cool blue stone in her mood ring.

"Do you want to leave?" whispered Stephanie, which made Nova flinch because she'd forgotten where she was and that there were other people around. She shook her head and then hit herself in the temple one-two-three-four times to calm down.

"Nova?"

Nova shook her head again and wrapped her arms protectively around NASA Bear and tried to pretend she could feel Bridget there beside her. She wouldn't leave now for all of the rings around Saturn.

Above them and all around, the stars froze in place. Nova was now viewing the night sky as it might appear out the circular window at the end of the attic after the streetlights clicked out. As suddenly as they had stopped, the stars began to move again, this time all to the left as if being spun on a globe, getting blurry until finally coming back into focus.

Mr. Mindy spoke from somewhere in the pitch-black center of the room.

"Here is where we left off last week."

A neon-green line formed in the sky, connecting a series of stars almost straight above the center of the room.

"Ursa Major: the Great Bear. One of the constellations

we can see from our homes throughout most of the year, if it's dark enough outside, Ursa Major is the third-largest . . ."

Nova could not concentrate on his voice and the room around her at the same time. She still couldn't quite breathe but she wasn't panicking either. She remembered the word Francine had used with Principal Dowling: "Overwhelmed." That was it, Nova realized. She felt overwhelmed. She took in air and her lungs expelled it but it felt like her heart had grown three sizes . . . like the heart of the Grinch in one of Francine's Dr. Seuss bedtime stories.

The rest of the class faded away again. Stephanie was gone. Zach Zbornak was gone. Mr. Mindy was gone.

Even Bridget was gone.

And Nova was floating.

She held on tight to NASA Bear, afraid he might drift away due to lack of gravity, but he didn't seem to be having the same breathing difficulties she was. Probably because of his space helmet. He was safe anywhere in the known universe.

The stars in the room swirled again.

"Hydra," a faraway voice was saying. "The largest constellation, named for a many-headed serpent in Greek mythology . . ."

In her head, Nova heard the voice of David Bowie.

"And the stars look very different today . . ."

For the second time in under ten minutes, her eyes filled with tears. She saw a shooting star above, so she made a wish. She wished the door would open and her sister would burst in. Bridget had never been to a planetarium either. If she had, surely she would have said so. Experiencing this magic without Bridget felt funny, but not the fun kind of funny. The bad kind of funny. Nova winced and wriggled as the funny feeling tugged at her tummy.

Nova bit her lip and hugged NASA Bear so hard his stuffing must've hurt.

"Cool, right?" whispered Stephanie.

The faraway voice hummed on, lecturing about this constellation and that. Nova covered her ears, choosing to listen to "Space Oddity" instead.

"And the stars look very different today . . ."

Another constellation.

Another neon-green line connecting the stars.

And another.

And another.

Words from the faraway voice invaded her brain. "Orion, Aries, Gemini, Leo, Lyra . . ."

Too soon, the lamp in the center of the room flicked on. The stars above and all around them went dark. Nova frowned.

"Next week's assignment . . . ," Mr. Mindy began. Nova tuned him out while Stephanie jotted the information down in her notebook. After what seemed like an eternity, the astronomy teacher again extinguished the lamp. "For the last couple minutes of class, let's sit back and enjoy . . ." He dragged out that last word, grinning, and didn't finish his sentence, much to Nova's annoyance.

"Enjoy what?" called out one of the boys, impatient.

"I'm sitting back!" another boy shouted.

"Don't leave us hanging, Mr. Mindy!" added a third.

Nova wondered if they would be scolded for not raising hands, but Mr. Mindy kept right on grinning, twirling his beard.

"Let's sit back and enjoy . . . a meteor shower!"

He flipped a switch.

Twinkling and blinking, getting brighter and dimmer, shooting stars enveloped Nova and NASA Bear, streaking across the sky. Out of the corner of her eye, Nova thought she caught a glimpse of the Little Prince, riding by on his asteroid planet. She squealed and bounced and flapped in her seat, unable to control her excitement, happier than she'd been since before Bridget went away.

Joanie was right.

It was amazing.

In her head, the voice of David Bowie swelled, louder and louder, until his voice was all she could hear.

"And the stars look very different today . . ."

Bridget had said the space shuttle *Challenger* gave them something to hope for.

"Nova, don't you see? The First Teacher in Space

contest shows us that anyone can have a dream! If they work hard enough and want it bad enough, anyone can escape Earth, even a high school social studies teacher from New Hampshire."

Escape was very important to Bridget.

"First, we escape foster care," she used to say. "Then, we escape New Hampshire. Next, we escape America, and finally, planet Earth. In outer space, surrounded by stars, there's no social worker to separate us. In outer space, dodging asteroids, there's no belly of the sheep. In outer space, approaching the moon, there's no radio static! There's no Vietnam War or kids starving in Ethiopia or mean teachers or foster families who pretend they want us but don't keep us forever! When *Challenger* sends Christa McAuliffe into space, Super Nova, we'll go too, but in our *minds*. It'll be good practice for when we're grown-ups, when we can get there for real. Just you and me and NASA Bear, our space shuttle, and the moon."

There was one more thing, thought Nova. One more amazing thing Bridget hadn't even considered.

Sound could not travel in space. In space, there wouldn't be the constant scratching of sounds that invaded her brain, making her want to bounce or scream or cover her ears. The only sounds would be from Ground Control and Bridget, radioed straight into her helmet, and "Space Oddity" by David Bowie, playing inside her head.

No cat-scratch pencils. No heating vents. No chattering kids.

Just Bridget and Bowie and Ground Control.

Nova's eyes filled with tears for the third time since the start of X-Block. She held her breath and hit herself in the temple one-two-three-four times but did not take her eyes off the twinkling flashes of falling meteors above and all around. Suddenly the stars stilled, and the moon was visible, closer than it could ever be seen from Earth, almost close enough to reach out and touch.

In six days, this would be the real-life view shared by the First Teacher in Space and the six other crew members of the space shuttle *Challenger*.

In six days, Bridget would be back.

6

JAN 22, 1986

Dear Bridget,

T-minus six days until *Challenger* launch.

I went to my first astronomy class in the planetarium today.

It is the best thing ever, Bridget. Everything Joanie said it would be. NASA Bear liked it too. He did not want to leave. The only bad part was that you were not there with us.

While we were walking upstairs, the girl who is helping me told me where my name comes from. Not the story you told me, about why you picked it and why it was perfect.

She told me about supernovas.

A supernova is the name for a star when it explodes. That's me. An exploding star.

After the planetarium, I could not think about school anymore. All I could think about was winning a contest and going to space and seeing a supernova up close and listening to "Space Oddity" and laughing with the stars.

Can I tell you a secret, Bridget? Not a big secret, like the Fox's secret. Just a little secret.

Here it is:

Even though Billy and Francine let me watch TV after school, I miss when we had to sneak it. I miss when we had to stay up late being real quiet so we would not get caught out of bed. I miss when we had to tiptoe down to the living room in our pajamas to watch Christa McAuliffe on *The Tonight Show Starring Johnny Carson*, with the volume turned down almost all the way.

"If you're offered a seat on a rocket ship," Christa McAuliffe told Johnny Carson, "don't ask what seat. Just get on."

"No duh!" you said. Remember? You said "No duh!" and you laughed so I laughed and we both laughed so loud it woke up our foster mother and she sent us back to bed but even after she yelled at us I couldn't stop laughing. NASA Bear was laughing too.

I miss that time for just us. I miss having a sister secret.

Here is another secret, Bridget:

I want to remember your eyes, but I can't.

I can't remember what color they were or the way they were shaped.

I can't remember whether you had sleepy swollen bags under them the way Joanie complains she does. I can't remember if you had laugh lines on the sides like Billy says Francine does. I can't remember if they were the same as my eyes or different.

I can't remember you smiling at me with your eyes, or winking, or blinking, or crossing them in a silly way, or rolling them up to the ceiling.

At school, Miss Chambers makes me look at her eyes. I hate it. I hate doing it, but I know what her eyes look like because I have to look over and over and over again when she says my name. Her eyes are plain boring brown and she wears Crayola Thistle eye shadow over the lids all the way to her eyebrows, which is weird. I try not to look too long.

Tonight at dinner, I looked at Billy and Francine's eyes. Not while they were looking at me. Never while they were looking. But when they looked away, when they looked at Joanie or at their food, I checked their eyes. I like their eyes more than Miss Chambers's eyes.

Francine's are Crayola Midnight Blue like the deepest part of the ocean when the sun's going down, way out where you could swim and not see your feet beneath you but you would know they are there, helping you tread water above the coral and rocks and sand and sharks and fishes and whales, not murky like pond water or clear like bath water. Dark, true, Midnight Blue.

Billy's eyes are Crayola Raw Umber, the brown of my favorite kind of mud, the kind that squishes squishily between your fingers when you play in the woods after the rain, the kind of mud that feels refrigerator cool even on the hottest summer day, completely pure without twigs or leaves or worms. Perfect, deep, Raw Umber.

Billy and Francine smile with their eyes. They wink and blink but do not cross them at me like Alex when he's being silly or roll them up like Mallory when she's in trouble. Billy always wears glasses. Francine never wears Thistle eye shadow.

They do not make me look at them, but I looked today. I looked at everyone's eyes today.

Alex's eyes are Crayola Cornflower Blue, a baby blanket blue.

Mallory's eyes are Crayola Forest Green, a Christmas tree green.

Joanie's eyes are Crayola Raw Sienna, a fluffy bunny brown.

Francine's are Midnight Blue and Billy's are Raw Umber.

I even looked in the mirror, Bridget. I looked for a long time.

My eyes are Crayola Sepia, a Lincoln Log brown.

When I could not remember yours, I opened the bedside table where I keep *The Little Prince*. Under the book is your photographs folder. There are five pictures of you in there. One of you by yourself on a beach, one of you and that boy from the movies, one of you with your high school friends, and two of us together. In the beach picture and the one with your friends, you are wearing sunglasses. In the picture with the boy, you are both wearing baseball caps. And in one of the pictures of us together, the one from last year, your eyes are closed because you're laughing.

The fifth and final photograph is from Mama's house. You are sitting on a couch with me in your arms. I am a baby wrapped in a blue blanket. You have your curly hair in pigtails and you are smiling with missing teeth. I don't know who took the picture but I know it wasn't Mama because she is kneeling on the floor in front of the couch with her back to the camera, holding her hand up under my body like she thinks you might drop me, which is silly because you would never let me go.

I love this picture, but it is old and yellowed and faded like you left it in the sun too long, and it did not answer my question at all.

What color are your eyes, Bridget?

Do we have the same eyes?

I need to see. I need to know.

I miss you.

Love,
Your Super Nova

Chapter Six

In the afternoon, Mr. O'Reilly told the class he had a surprise for everyone.

"Principal Dowling has arranged for every kid in our whole school to be able to watch the upcoming launch of the space shuttle *Challenger*!"

Nova twitched in her seat. Miss Chambers shot her a knowing smile.

"Seventh and eighth grades will go to the auditorium, but sixth graders will watch in your classrooms. We're going to wheel in one of the rainy-day-recess TVs and cable network CNN will broadcast it for kids across America. Now, who can tell me what's special about *Challenger*?"

Nova wriggled and squeaked. She raised her hand, the way Mr. O'Reilly was always reminding kids to do if they shouted out answers. He saw her hand and nodded, but then he pointed to a frizzy-haired girl in the front row.

"Julia?"

"NASA and President Reagan held a big contest to find someone to be the First Teacher in Space and the one they picked will teach lessons from on board the shuttle."

"That's right!" Mr. O'Reilly high-fived her. "Can anyone tell me what state the winning teacher is from?"

This time, Nova put up two hands. But Zach Zbornak shouted out his answer without raising even one.

"She's from here! New Hampshire!"

"That's right, Zach! But don't forget to raise your hand."

"Who went to space first?" asked Front Row Julia. "Was it Buzz Aldrin?"

RUSSIA! Nova wanted to scream. The first person in space was a Russian named Yuri Gagarin.

"Guhguhguhguhguh!" she cried, unable to pronounce the cosmonaut's last name. She wanted to add that Alan Shepard, the first American astronaut in space, had been from New Hampshire, just like them. Just like Christa McAuliffe. "Nuh-ha! Mm!"

"Nova, let's settle down, please. You're getting a little loud," said Miss Chambers softly. Nova glanced around. Her classmates were staring at her, including Mallory and Mary-Beth.

"Class? Eyes up here!" ordered Mr. O'Reilly. "Which country went into space first?" He pointed at a tall boy in the back. "Winslow?"

"Uh . . . America?"

Nova grunted and slapped her hands down on the desk. Why hadn't Mr. O'Reilly called on *her*? She knew it was not America!

"Nope! Russia beat us by a few weeks! That cosmonaut's name was Yuri Gagarin. Write that down."

Mallory, Mary-Beth, and the rest of the kids who could take notes picked up their pencils.

"Now, does anyone here have any idea how a space shuttle gets off the ground?"

"Ah-ah-ah-mm!" shouted Nova. She stood, raised one hand again, and smacked the desktop one-two-three-four times with the other. Bridget had taught her all about how a space shuttle works by shooting fuel out of the bottom so hard and fast it's the pressure against the earth that launches it into orbit. It takes off like a rocket but lands like an airplane.

"I know you're excited, Nova," whispered Miss Chambers, tugging her arm, "and I love that excitement! But you need a quiet voice and happy hands, or we'll have to leave the room."

Nova flopped back down, clenched her fists, and had a quiet voice as Mr. O'Reilly explained to the class all the stuff she already knew, all the information Bridget had copied from library books and brought home to her over the years. Her favorites were about the planets and stars.

"You know, Nova," Bridget had said once, reading from her notes, "some of the stars we see twinkling in the sky probably burned out a long time ago. It takes their light *at least* four years to reach our eyes on Earth, so you and me have no way of knowing when they've already gone dark. That's why, when you wish on one, you should wish on two more too, just to be sure. You don't want to waste a wish on a star that's already dead."

Nova closed her eyes and set her forehead down on the desk while Mr. O'Reilly continued to ask and answer questions about space travel. She knew all the answers.

But nobody asked her.

★ ★ ★

"Check out what I got!" Bridget opened her Trapper Keeper, a gift from their latest foster mother. They were sitting on the floor of their bedroom, wearing their warmest pajamas and drinking hot cocoa. It was noon on a Tuesday, but an early-December snowstorm had canceled school. Nova was ten and Bridget was a high school sophomore, and they were with a brand-new foster family. Again.

"I would have showed you yesterday, but with Mrs. Steele here all afternoon, I totally forgot!"

"Bidge!" Nova slapped her forehead, like the people in the commercial who could have had a V8. Bridget laughed. She didn't mind being teased about her forgetfulness.

"I know, I'm sorry!" Bridget placed the Trapper Keeper in Nova's lap. "This is Sally Ride. She's my hero." There was a glossy magazine photo on the inside front cover, featuring a woman with short, curly dark hair wearing a black shirt with the NASA logo on the front, just like on NASA Bear's suit. She was floating inside a space shuttle, wearing a headset. Smiling.

"You remember about Sally Ride, right? She just went to space in June, the first American woman ever, and she's going back next year! My physics teacher gave me this article about her. The news reporters asked her all sorts of ridiculous questions because she's a woman, like if she cries when things go wrong and what kind of makeup she planned to travel with, can you believe that? In this interview, she says as a kid she took all the science classes she could, so that's what I'll do too. What *we'll* do. And it wasn't easy. She went to an all-girls school where they didn't really focus on science or advanced math or chemistry or physics, so she had to keep learning and learning. She went to college for her bachelor's, then earned her master's, then got her PhD. Know why? It's because being an astronaut doesn't just happen, Nova. You have to *want* it and you have to *work* at it."

Bridget wanted it. Bridget was working at it.

Nova wanted to work at it too.

★ ★ ★

"Nova? Hey, Nova!" It was Mallory's voice, interrupting Nova's memory. "Earth to Nova! It's your turn. Give it a spin!"

Nova shook her head one-two-three-four times. She'd forgotten what they were doing. She'd forgotten they were playing a game.

"Here!" Mallory put her hand over Nova's and made her spin the Chutes and Ladders spinner while Buddy, Mary-Beth, and Alex waited. Nova pulled her hand away. She did not like hands touching her hands, not even Mallory's hands. She picked up her game piece.

"Good job!" said Mallory as Nova moved four spaces. "You're on space nine! You mowed the lawn! Now go up the ladder."

"You in the lead!" exclaimed Alex. "That means you's winning!"

Nova smiled.

She liked winning.

But whenever it wasn't her turn, she let her brain go right back to Bridget.

5

JAN 23, 1986

Dear Bridget,

T-minus five days until *Challenger* launch.

This afternoon at school was good, then bad, then good again.

The first good thing was in Mr. O'Reilly's room. He said we will watch the *Challenger* launch from our classroom on the TV, which means we will not miss it.

The bad thing was when he asked questions about space and no one let me tell the answers. They want me to sit with a Quiet Voice and a Calm Body and Happy Hands and just listen! It's not fair. When you come to watch the launch, you can tell Mr. O'Reilly and Miss Chambers how smart I am so he will call on me and she will not say "Please settle down."

After that, the afternoon got good again. I played Chutes and Ladders with Mallory and Alex and Buddy and Mary-Beth . . . and I won! I was the first one to make it all the way to the blue ribbon 100 square. I beat Mallory by only one because she was on 99 and Alex says

99 plus 1 equals 100. When I got to 100 Mallory said a bad word and threw her game piece and then knocked the board on the floor so Miss Chambers made her go sit down. She stomped her feet and ripped up the rules reminder sheet hanging next to her desk. Mary-Beth says Mallory does not like to lose. But she must have stopped being mad by the end of the day, because she asked me and Buddy to play Play-Doh with her.

When Buddy is not bouncing, he likes to make face pieces with the Play-Doh, like Mr. Potato Head has, then he puts them on his own face. Today he made blue straight line eyebrows and placed them on his forehead, almost touching in the center but up on the ends, to look angry. He frowned hard and wagged his pointer finger, looking just like the guy helper teacher when he is giving directions for the tenth time. Mallory snorted.

"Oh, hello, Mr. Malone!" she said. "When did you get here?"

Buddy laughed and took the Play-Doh off his face, leaving it balled up in front of him. He tapped the back of Mallory's hand and pointed to her face.

"Okay, my turn. Who am I?" She put on a yellow Play-Doh beard and mustache. "It Is Especially Special To See You Looking So Special Today, Special Ed Kids!"

I laughed my biggest laugh because I knew who she

was right away: Principal Dowling, who says every word like it's its own sentence!

"Your turn, Nova." She handed me a ball of green, but I did not know who to be. Buddy took it out of my hand and made two circles, which he attached together with a curved line. He pressed them around my eyes.

"Glasses," said Mallory. "Are you Miss Chambers?"

That gave me an idea. I picked up Buddy's hand and made him wave it the right way, like Miss Chambers did to me on Day One. Then I told him "Touch blue," but I didn't think he would get it because it sounded like "Tuh boo."

"Boo!" said Buddy. He smashed the rolled-up blue Play-Doh and laughed.

"You sounded just like her!" said Mallory. "You're so funny, Nova!"

And then Francine was there to take me home.

After school, Billy came home from work early and asked me and Joanie to make cookies with him. Joanie said no because she is busy studying for when she goes back to college, but I love making cookies! Billy is a good baker like Mama was.

"Dad doesn't get to bake fun stuff like that at his restaurant," said Joanie. "He supervises the chefs while they make fancy snails and duck pâté!"

I stuck out my tongue. I have not been to Billy's restaurant yet. Francine says it is very fancy and always busy, but if the chefs are making snails and ducks I don't want to go!

"Dad's restaurant works with a community organization that helps people with Down syndrome and autism get jobs," added Joanie. "It's a pretty cool place. And the mushroom risotto is . . ." She put two thumbs up.

I stuck my tongue out again because mushrooms belong in the ground, not on my plate. Then Joanie went back to her books and Billy went back to the baking.

"Will you crack these for me, Nova?" Billy asked when it was egg time.

I tried.

But I guess I did not do my best job because the egg fell apart and shells went in the bowl and then I thought maybe I might cry. I bit my hand between my thumb and pointer finger.

"It's okay!" Billy took my hand out of my mouth. He used a big part of the shell to get the little bits of shell out. "I'll teach you. Practice makes perfect!"

He held his hand over my hand and we tap-tap-tapped the egg on the edge of the bowl to make a line in the shell. He held my hands in his hands and helped me pull the two sides apart so the Yellow-Orange yolk and gooey

clear part fell in the bowl with no shell pieces. He let me
do the next one myself and this time I did a good job. No
shells went in.

Then he showed me how to use the electric mixer, which
I kind of did not like because it was loud but also kind of
liked because of the way the silver beaters swirled round
and round and round. After we put in everything except
the chocolate chips he let me eat some raw dough but not
while Francine was in the kitchen because Billy says she
does not allow that. He looked at Joanie.

"Don't worry, I won't tell!" She was sitting at the table,
reading a boring-looking book, writing notes, and eating
carrots. "I'd have some too but I'm trying to eat healthier."

"Yeah," said Billy. "If your mother asks, I am too." Then
he took a big bite of the raw dough.

I do not remember if Mama let me eat raw dough,
but I remember baking with her when you were at school.
I remember one time we made brownies and another
time we made a whole chocolate cake with white frosting
with pink flowers. I remember standing on a chair and
I remember a wooden spoon and I remember Mama
singing along with the radio and calling me her special girl.
I remember the time I spilled the whole bag of flour and I
cried but Mama laughed and then we drew hearts in the
powder on the floor until you got home from school and

made us clean it up; like you were the mama and Mama
was the big sister.

I have not thought about that in a long long long time.

I want you to bake with Billy and me.

Is it okay if I like baking with Billy?

When the cookies were in the oven, I went upstairs to
my room, found our old astronaut toy, picked up NASA
Bear, got your mix tape and Walkman, and went up to
the attic.

Even though you have taped over Side B many many
many times with new music by Michael Jackson and
Madonna, thank you for keeping Side A the same. I like
that it is the same. I like knowing what song will be next.
I like that when I listen to them, all my bad thoughts
go away.

I rewound the tape to the beginning and pressed Play
for David Bowie to sing "Space Oddity." I needed to
hear about Major Tom leaving his wife behind on Earth
to travel into space. I put NASA Bear in my lap to be
Ground Control and pretended the astronaut was Major
Tom while I waited for the countdown. I closed my eyes to
imagine I was there. Just like you taught me whenever I
needed to forget about missing Mama.

But the Walkman wasn't working.

And I started to cry.

I've been crying a lot since you've been gone, Bridget.
I try to be tough like you, but I'm not you. So I sat there
and I cried and I didn't know what to do, and then the
door opened, the overhead light came on, and there was
Joanie.

"Nova! I went looking for you in your room and you
were gone! Then I opened the door to the attic and heard
crying. Are you okay? Did you hurt yourself?"

I held up the Walkman.

"Did you drop it? Is it broken?" Joanie sat cross-legged
beside me. "Doesn't look broken." She opened it to check
the tape. "Looks okay."

I shook my head. Not okay.

"Can I see?" She reached for the headphones. I let her
take them. She put them on her ears and pressed Play.
"No sound? I bet it's the batteries. Don't cry! I've got more
in my room. Come downstairs."

I followed Joanie down to her room. Her room is . . . pink.
All shades.

The walls are Crayola Salmon pink, her bedspread is
Mulberry and Magenta, her curtains are neon pink, and
her carpet is pale pink. All that pink kind of made me
feel like I was standing inside county fair cotton candy,
and my tummy twisted. I have not had cotton candy since
last Halloween.

"Here you go!" Joanie placed two new batteries inside the back of the Walkman, popped it shut, and handed it to me. "Good as new!"

I said "Ah" but I meant "Thanks," and then I left to go back to the attic, but now I wasn't thinking about Major Tom. I was thinking about last Halloween.

You said you were taking me trick-or-treating.

That was a lie.

It was not the first time you lied to our foster parents, but it was the first time you lied to me.

We went to that boy's house for a party instead, even though our foster parents always said "No parties!" and "No boys!"

You made our costumes. Yours was pointy cardboard ears glued to a headband with a fluffy brown and white tail. Mine was a mint-green one-piece jumpsuit with a yellow scarf.

You knocked on the boy's door. I held out my pillowcase. I wanted my candy.

He opened the door and smiled with too many teeth. He was not holding a candy bowl like people are supposed to on Halloween, but he was in costume, a long black cape with his face painted white with red drips by the corners of his mouth. You shrieked and jumped back.

"Ahh! Look, Nova! A vampire!"

He laughed and took his teeth out. That's when I jumped back. Teeth are not supposed to come out. He showed them to me.

"Fake fangs. What do you think?"

You said, "Nova likes them. She thinks they're cool."

But that was another lie.

I did not like them. I thought they were gross. Then you asked if he liked our costumes.

"You're a cat and she's . . . an elf?" he guessed.

That made me mad, even madder than not getting candy when he opened the door.

"I'm the Fox and she's the Little Prince! Geez, read a book sometime, you troglodyte!"

"You're the foxiest fox I've ever seen!" he said. Then he hugged you. "Come in. Everyone's already here." We followed him to the kitchen, where a chicken, a roll of Life Savers, Batman, Wonder Woman, two cats in short dresses, and a wrestler were all crowded around a bowl of candy on the table, but none of them were saying "Trick or treat!" before they took some.

"Check it out!" said the boy, pointing to a machine on the counter. "I rented it. It makes cotton candy! Cool, huh?"

"So cool!" you said. "Right, Nova?"

I crossed my arms and did not speak.

Then you asked me to please be good so I said "Mm"

and you said thank you, but I didn't mean yes. I meant mad. I was mad. I was mad because I wanted to trick-or-treat and I was mad because you lied. I stayed mad for almost the whole party. I stayed mad even while I was eating my cotton candy. I ate so much cotton candy my stomach hurt.

But after everyone else had gone, I heard you talking to that boy.

He said, "It must be a lot of work, bringing Nova everywhere. Won't it be nice to go to college without her?"

You said, "No. I won't go anywhere without her. Not even college."

He laughed. "Come on. Aren't you always telling me you have to get out of that house, out of this town? They're not just gonna let you take her with you when you turn eighteen. You know that, right?"

Then you said, "I don't care what they say. If I can take her to the moon, I can take her anywhere."

Suddenly, I wasn't mad anymore.

I miss you.

Love,
Your Super Nova

Chapter Seven

Friday started the same as Thursday and Wednesday and Tuesday and Monday. Nova sat at her desk half-heartedly participating in Mrs. Pierce's testing, trying to balance her teacher's voice with all of the other noises both in the room and in her head. It was not easy. She did not do well. Nova thought about Francine telling her to do her best job and tried to work harder, but it was impossible. She found herself wondering what would happen if she did her worst job instead, if she didn't even try. Would Francine and Billy give her back to foster care? When Bridget stopped doing well in school, when she stopped trying and told everyone she didn't care about the rules or her grades anymore, their last foster family threatened to send her away. They said they couldn't handle her anymore. That was why she wanted to escape.

"We might have to be apart for a little while, Nova,"

she'd said. "They might separate us again, but if they do, I'll come back for you. I'll be back before the *Challenger* launches so we can watch it together, like we planned, no matter what. I promise."

* * *

The first time they got separated, almost one whole year ago, Nova was scared. She and Bridget had never been apart before, not overnight, not even one time, but all of a sudden Nova was in a group home for special kids and Bridget was someplace else, and nobody told her why or for how long they'd be apart. Every night, after she was tucked in, Nova would sneak out of bed and go to the window to find the three brightest stars and wish for Bridget to find her. It took a long time, from before Valentine's Day to after Easter, but finally Nova got her wish.

It was a Tuesday afternoon when Mrs. Steele, their social worker, picked Nova up at school. She talked to the teacher for a few minutes, then turned to Nova and said, "I have a surprise for you!"

When they got out to Mrs. Steele's wood-paneled station wagon, there was Bridget, grinning in the backseat. Nova jumped and squeaked and crawled in beside her. Then they hugged and hugged and Bridget promised she would never let them get split up again. Mrs.

Steele drove a long way to their new home, where they had hot oatmeal, warm blankets, and two sets of bunk beds. The new foster parents did not allow loud music or TV or caffeine, but Nova didn't care about any of their silly rules. She was just happy to be back with Bridget.

"You knew I'd get us back together, right, Nova?" Bridget asked before bedtime that first night. "You weren't too scared? You knew I'd fix it."

"Mm!" said Nova, pulling NASA Bear out of her backpack and handing him to her sister.

"I missed this guy too." Bridget kissed his soft plastic helmet. "You know, Mama gave him to me when I turned three. That means he's older than you are!"

"Na-ah Beah." Nova tapped her sister's hand with NASA Bear's paw. She wanted Bridget to know he'd missed her too.

"I can't believe they put you in a group home. Me too, by the way. I was in one for teens." Bridget dropped her voice so the girls in the other set of bunk beds couldn't hear. "That rotten Mrs. Steele said it was temporary, just until they found a house to take us both, but I'll never let that happen again, okay?"

"Kay-kay."

"*Oh*-kay?"

"*Oh-kay.*"

"I mean it." Bridget held one of Nova's hands between hers. Nova did not pull away. "Even if they put us in different states—no, different countries . . . No, different planets!—even if they put us on different *planets,* I'll still find a way to get back to you. I promise."

★ ★ ★

For the first time, it occurred to Nova that if she didn't know where to send Bridget's letters, how would Bridget know where to find her? A sick feeling twisted up in her gut. She would have to wish on three bright stars that Bridget already knew about Billy and Francine.

But even if Bridget *did* know about Billy and Francine, what if Mrs. Steele moved Nova again before the launch? What if the Wests decided they didn't want a girl who didn't do her best job during testing? What if they couldn't handle her anymore?

What if Bridget arrived at Jefferson Middle School to find that Nova was gone? Nova bit down hard on her lip, shook her head one-two-three-four times, and tried her hardest to concentrate on what Mrs. Pierce was asking her to do, but with tears stinging her eyes it was hard to see the blocks she was supposed to be stacking.

Later in Mr. O'Reilly's room, Nova and Mary-Beth colored maps of the United States while the rest of the class talked about Russia's iron curtains, then all the girls lined up like ducklings to go to home economics while the boys went down to woodshop.

"Welcome, welcome, class!" The home economics teacher ushered them in. Nova liked her right away. She looked like Strega Nona, that old lady from the picture book, short and plump with gray hair, a long apron, a huge nose, and an oversized bosom that prompted Nova to glance down at her own flat chest and wonder if she would ever fill out like Bridget had in middle school. She placed her hands over her nonexistent boobs, checking for signs of growth. Nothing.

"Nova!" snapped Miss Chambers. "Hands out of your overalls!"

Standing a little to the left of them, two girls could barely hold back their giggles. One looked at Nova, then whispered to the other behind her hand.

Nova removed her palms from her chest, confused and embarrassed. She hit herself one-two-three-four times in the temple with her palm to make the bad feeling go away, but it did not work. What were the girls laughing about? Why did Miss Chambers seem upset?

"Those girls are super mean," hissed Mallory, adjusting her glasses and glaring at them. "Last semester one of their friends tripped Mary-Beth in gym class. She said it was an accident but it was no accident."

"We're baking chocolate chip cookies today!" announced Not-Strega-Nona, clapping her hands together. "Your materials have already been set out."

Miss Chambers beamed at Mallory, Mary-Beth, and Nova. Nova grinned back. She could bake cookies! She could crack eggs! She wondered if they would be allowed to eat the raw dough.

The thirteen girls were separated into three groups at three workstations, with two ovens in each workstation and two girls at each oven, except for the one Nova, Mary-Beth, and Mallory were to use with Miss Chambers.

Sharing their workstation were the two giggling girls, who were not giggling anymore.

"Great, we're at the spaz station!" said the taller girl, who Nova thought looked like a carrot thanks to her bright orange dress, ginger hair, and wide green cloth headband. She was the one who had been pointing. "Can't Denise and me work with Ashley and Sammy Jo?"

"No, Krystle," said Not-Strega-Nona. "I let you choose your partners, not your stations."

Carrot Krystle let out an exaggerated sigh as her friend, whose hair was pulled into dozens of braids, shrugged. She was wearing a polka-dot dress with matching plastic jewelry. Nova decided to name her Polka Dot Denise.

While Not-Strega-Nona lectured on the importance of safety in the work space, Nova felt herself drifting away. Her eyes saw stars. Her ears heard music. She covered her ears to block out the teacher so "Space Oddity" filled the room. She pictured herself standing on a planet, alone, like the Little Prince, waiting for the Fox to come with his secret.

"Nova?" Miss Chambers nudged her gently. "Nova, it's time to start."

Nova lowered her hands. She had missed all the instructions. But that was okay. Cookies were easy.

Nova, Mallory, and Mary-Beth took turns measuring, pouring, and mixing, led by Miss Chambers, who wouldn't let them eat any of the raw dough but did look the other way when they snuck a few chocolate chips. When Miss Chambers asked for a volunteer to crack the eggs, Nova jumped and squeaked and raised her hand. She did the job carefully. Tap-tap-tap. No shells in the bowl. She wished she could tell Billy.

While Nova was cracking, Mary-Beth was looking for a pot holder, for later. She found one and pulled it off the counter between the two workstations, not realizing the other girls' carton of eggs was resting on its corner. The carton crashed to the floor, spilling egg yolk.

"Oh, great!" said Carrot Krystle. "Look what you did!"

"It wath an accthident," whispered Mary-Beth. Her whole face went Carnation Pink as her eyes filled with tears. Mary-Beth cried easily, even more easily than Nova.

"Be more careful, then!" snapped Carrot Krystle. She knelt on the floor to clean up. Miss Chambers insisted that Mary-Beth help, then reminded Carrot Krystle to be nice before hurrying away to get more paper towels from the dispenser by the door.

Carrot Krystle wrinkled her nose as if the eggs smelled bad.

"It's not fair, Denise! Why are they even in our class? One's a spaz"—she glared at Mary-Beth—"one's a creep"—she shot a look at Mallory—"and the new girl makes weird noises."

"Don't worry, Nova." Mallory's voice was so low Nova almost didn't hear her even though they were standing shoulder to shoulder. "We'll get them back good."

Nova did not understand what that meant.

"I actually feel bad for the new girl." Polka Dot Denise was staring sympathetically at Nova. "I mean, it's not her fault she makes weird noises. She's probably retarded."

Carrot Krystle nodded as she tossed the sopping paper towels in the trash. "Yup. Can't even talk. Definitely a retard."

Nova's cheeks burned. She wished Bridget was here to say "My sister's not dumb. She's a thinker, not a talker."

Except Bridget was gone.

And Nova was "probably retarded."

"Soon," whispered Mallory. "So soon . . ."

Nova rubbed her hands up and down her arms. Mallory's growled words had given her goose bumps.

Miss Chambers returned. She helped Krystle and Mary-Beth get the last of the gooey egg off the floor.

"Mallory, how about you put the cookies in the oven?" asked Miss Chambers. Mallory did. "Excellent! Now we wait!"

Beside them, Carrot Krystle was putting her cookie sheet in the oven she shared with Polka Dot Denise.

"Miss Chambers, Mary-Beth has to go to the bathroom." Mallory elbowed Mary-Beth hard in the ribs. "Don't you?"

"Yeth," Mary-Beth agreed. She crossed her legs at the knee.

"Looks like she's gotta go bad," said Mallory. "Better hurry!"

"Come on." Miss Chambers took Mary-Beth's hand. "Girls, do not touch this stove while we're gone. Very important. Safety first, right?"

Mallory smiled. "We won't touch this stove."

"Or the oven."

Mallory smiled bigger. "Or *this* oven."

As soon as they were out of the room, Mallory whispered in Nova's ear again.

"It's time."

Nova screwed up her face, confused. *Time for what?*

"You distract them."

Nova did not react.

"That means you do something to make them look at you."

Nova did not react.

"You go stand over there and scream your biggest scream."

Nova did not react.

"Go!" Mallory pushed her toward the center of the room. "Scream. I'll take care of the rest."

Nova walked ten steps. She took a big breath. She turned. Mallory nodded.

Nova screamed.

Everyone in class stopped what they were doing to look at her. She did not like it, so many people looking. She covered her ears and squinted. She wanted to disappear.

Behind Carrot Krystle and Polka Dot Denise, Mallory was fiddling with the knob on the oven. She shot Nova a thumbs-up and gestured for her to come back. Nova sprinted back to her station, trying to forget the feeling of all those eyes on her.

"Keep working, class," said Not-Strega-Nona pleasantly. "Everything's fine!"

"Miss Chambers said not to touch *this* oven." Mallory smirked. "She didn't say anything about *that* oven."

"Ehh?" asked Nova, meaning "Why?" Mallory, somehow, seemed to understand.

"Those girls are mean. I don't like them calling Mary-Beth a spaz and I don't like them calling you a retard. You are my friends, and I don't let *anybody* be mean to my friends."

"Ah," said Nova. She liked being called a friend.

Ten minutes after Mary-Beth and Miss Chambers returned, a timer beeped. Miss Chambers helped Mary-Beth take out the cookies so they could cool. On the other side of the workstation, Carrot Krystle was sniffing the air.

"Does something smell . . . funny?" she asked.

"Pretty funny," said Mallory in that low voice that gave Nova goose bumps.

"It smells like . . . like something's burning," said Polka Dot Denise.

"Oh, no!" Carrot Krystle yanked down hard on the oven door. Black smoke came spiraling out, making her cough. Miss Chambers quickly closed the oven door with the charred cookies still inside and turned the dial to Off.

"They're ruined!" screeched Polka Dot Denise. "Krystle, *what did you do?*"

"Me? *I* didn't do anything!"

"The oven was on four fifty? You put it on four fifty?"

"No! You must have touched it when I wasn't looking!"

"Did not!"

"Did too!"

"Did not, you liar!"

"You must have, you . . . you . . . you *airhead*!" Carrot Krystle shoved her friend, hard.

"Nice one!" Polka Dot Denise pushed back. *"Not!"*

"Girls!" Not-Strega-Nona rushed over to break up the scuffle. She opened the oven just long enough to remove the smoldering cookie sheet, which she set on the stove. Several kids pinched their noses. Miss Chambers opened a window.

"Nasty!" said a tall freckle-faced girl. "Krystle, your cookies reek worse than a tire fire!"

"It's not my fault!" shouted Carrot Krystle.

"Too bad," said Mallory. "Even us *retards* know not to turn the oven up so high."

"You did this!" Carrot Krystle pointed at them.

"Don't be a jerk, Krystle!" said Polka Dot Denise. "They wouldn't."

Mallory picked up a perfect cookie from their tray and took a bite, then put a "shh" finger to her lips and winked at Nova. Nova grinned.

Just like the Little Prince and the Fox, now Nova and Mallory shared a secret.

4

JAN 24, 1986

Dear Bridget,

T-minus four days until *Challenger* launch.

Today some girls in school called me retarded. You were not there to yell at them. But it's okay. Mallory burnt their cookies and made them mad. You will like Mallory, I think. She is my friend. My first friend. I know because she told me, "I don't let anybody be mean to my friends."

I think maybe I should feel bad, Bridget, because I know burning their cookies was not nice. But I tried and I tried and I tried and I just don't feel bad. Does that mean I'm not nice?

Now I am worried.

What if Francine finds out? What if Francine wants to give me back because I'm not a nice girl? Francine told Mrs. Pierce I am a very nice girl. I don't feel like a nice girl. I feel mean. But I also feel happy because those girls were mean first and Mallory got them back good.

What is the word for when you feel two different feelings at the same time?

It feels like if one feeling was yellow and the other feeling was red but when you mixed them together instead of making orange they made something they shouldn't, like pine green. I feel Crayola Pine Green and that doesn't make sense.

Then, to make it worse, today on the drive home from school, Francine told me Mrs. Steele is coming this weekend to do her "wellness check." But you and me both know a "wellness check" is really a deciding visit so Mrs. Steele can see whether we should stay with our foster family or get moved to a new one. I don't want her to come.

Even though Francine thinks I cannot read, reads me Dr. Seuss at bedtime, and does not allow raw dough eating, I like her. And even though you say "We should not get attached" because "Foster families are not forever families," I want to stay.

She bought me seven pairs of overalls so I can wear overalls every day and she bought me slouch socks and she cut the tags out of the backs of all my shirts, and she asks me about my day and tells me about her day in the car on the way home from school, and she lets me watch TV when she braids my hair so I forget it hurts to get my hair braided.

Then I feel bad again because those are all the things you do, Bridget. Except buying overalls. You get me slouch socks and cut my tags out and ask about my day and tell me about your day and let me listen to David Bowie when you braid my hair so I forget it hurts, remember?

I like Francine and Billy, but I want you to read my bedtime stories.

And I like Mallory but I want you to share my secrets, like the Fox's secret.

I have so many confusing feelings I think they might fill me up like the expanding universe and then explode me out like a supernova. During testing today, I started to worry that you will not find me. But then I told myself, of course you will. You found me before, the last time they sent us to different foster homes, when we were apart for ten whole weeks. You found me then so I know you'll find me now. If NASA can find the way from the Earth to the moon, you can find your way from wherever you are to wherever I am! I need to stop worrying. I know you do not like for me to worry. I know you keep your promises.

Francine and Billy are nice, but they're not forever family. You are my forever family.

I miss you.

Love,
Your Super Nova

Chapter Eight

"It's almost here!" Billy held up the newspaper Saturday morning. There was another article about the upcoming *Challenger* launch with full-color pictures of the seven space shuttle crew members. "Hey, Nova, I forget . . . which one's going to be the First Teacher in Space? This guy with the handsome mustache?" Billy pointed to astronaut and physicist Ronald McNair, who had a mustache like Billy's and the same shade of brown skin, but unlike Billy, McNair wasn't bald.

Nova shook her head and giggled.

She pointed to Christa McAuliffe, who had Francine's light peach complexion and small nose, but her face was framed by curly brown hair with bangs, and she did not wear glasses.

McNair and McAuliffe were wearing Cornflower blue jackets with red-on-white NASA logo patches on the right, standing in front of the American flag.

The astronaut was holding his helmet while the teacher held a model space shuttle the length of a ruler which looked exactly like the one Bridget had drawn for Nova a million times, colored with Crayolas, when teaching her about space travel, except Bridget always wrote their last name, VEZINA, where it was supposed to say NASA.

In the pictures, Christa McAuliffe and Ronald Mc-Nair were smiling.

"Of course they're smiling," Bridget had said the first time she saw the pictures. "I'd be smiling so hard my cheeks would crack and crumble away!"

Nova hadn't thought cracked, crumbling cheeks would be worth smiling over, but she liked the picture anyway.

After Billy read the article, Nova, flapping cheerfully, started up the stairs. She wanted to watch cable TV. But Francine was rushing down.

"What's this?" she asked, holding out Nova's Letters to Bridget notebook, the one Mrs. Pierce had said was full of scribbles.

"Mm," said Nova, meaning "Mine," reaching for it. Francine didn't give it up.

"I found it when I was cleaning your room. It looks like writing. Have you been writing?"

"Mm," said Nova, this time meaning "Yes," reaching for it again.

"Look, Billy!" Francine opened the spiral-bound notebook and held it out to him. "Some of it is just scribbles, but this looks like *me*. And this word, this looks like *moon*. That one's almost definitely *Nova*. And here! This could be *ton*."

Ten, Nova wanted to say. *That word is not* ton; *it is* ten.

Only Bridget had ever been able to read Nova's note-book and even she got it wrong most of the time, though Nova always pretended her sister's guesses were right by nodding and saying "Mm!" a lot. She reached for it a third time. None of the words were "just scribbles." All of the words were meant for Bridget's eyes only.

"Can you read, Nova?" asked Billy. "Did Mrs. Pierce test her reading?"

"I don't know! Her last teacher's report said she doesn't even know the alphabet, but Mrs. Pierce is sup-posed to give me a full report when the testing is over. That's not for another week at least."

Another week *of testing?* Nova groaned. She wished she could talk so she could ask to be All Done.

"I have an idea!" exclaimed Francine. "Honey, grab me a Sharpie and construction paper. I need to find the scissors."

"Top drawer on the left with the can opener!" Billy hurried out to find the marker and paper.

Nova sat in the kitchen chair and rocked and hummed. She wanted her notebook back. And she wanted to watch TV. But once Francine had all the materials, she began to write and cut until she had created a long line of letters, the entire alphabet in order. Under it, she created two smaller strips, one with the letters *A E I O U* and one with *D L M R S T.*

"Vowels and some commonly used consonants," Francine explained to Billy. "My kindergarteners tend to recognize these ones first."

Kindergarten babies, thought Nova.

On the rest of the paper, which Francine cut to the size of index cards, she wrote several short words. *Cat. Hat. Dog. Boy. Moon. Me. Nova. Top. Red. No. Yes. Bridget.*

Nova's heart fluttered at that last one.

Now Francine was testing Nova, same as Mrs. Pierce. "Touch *A.* Touch *E.* Touch *R.* Touch *S.* Touch *L.*"

Nova tried to pay attention and do her best work as Francine added more and more consonants into the mix. She knew her letters when there were only five or ten to choose from, but as usual once she had the whole alphabet she mixed up *B* and *D* and *P.* She remembered *O* but didn't remember *Q,* and if she tried to go too fast, *M* looked like *N* and *N* looked like *M,* even though she knew *M* was for *Moon* and *N* was for *Nova.*

"Let's try these words next," said Francine.

"I'll get the camcorder!" exclaimed Billy. He left the kitchen and returned a moment later with a huge black video recorder propped up on his shoulder, red light on.

"Nova, give me *CAT.*"

Nova looked carefully at the cards. *CAT* was easy.

CAT began with *C*. *CAT* ended with *AT*. *CAT* was one of the first words Bridget had taught her to read. She handed Francine *CAT*.

"Great job!"

Nova blinked back tears. This felt just like school, like school testing, but at home, and what good could it do? Nova knew how testing ended.

Cannot read. Does not speak. Severely mentally retarded.

And once they determined that, maybe they wouldn't want her anymore. The last family hadn't wanted Bridget anymore when she was getting bad grades. Nova would be moved again. She would have to say goodbye to the attic window and raw cookie dough and her first-ever friends from Jefferson Middle School, and Bridget would not know where to find her.

"Nova, give me *HAT*."

Nova gave her *CAT*.

"No, Nova. Give me *HAT*. Hah-hah-hat."

Why is she saying it weird? Not making eye contact, Nova handed over *HAT*.

"Nova, give me *MOON*."

Nova couldn't help smiling. Without having to think twice, she grabbed *MOON* and placed it in Francine's outstretched hand. *MOON* was easy. *MOON*, she liked. Bridget had taught her *MOON* when she was five. She used to write it in the notebook while she was in the belly of the sheep, waiting for her sister to get home from school. Over and over. *Moon, moon, moon.* That was one of the words Nova could almost always read.

Francine kept rotating through the words, sometimes with the same word requested twice in a row, sometimes not. Sometimes Nova got them right, sometimes not. But more right than not. They went through all of the words except two.

"Nova, what is your name?" asked Francine. Nova was confused. Francine knew her name. She'd *just said* her name. Besides, how could Nova answer "What is your name?" When she had tried in kindergarten the word got stuck in her throat and all she could say was "Bidge Bidge Bidge," which got her in big trouble.

"Give me your name." Francine gestured toward the cards.

"Ah!" Nova squeaked, realizing she *could* answer that question. She picked up the card that said *NOVA* and handed it to Francine. She tapped her chest. "Mm!" She meant "Me."

"Great job, Nova!" cheered Billy, his face half-hidden by the huge video camera.

"Last one, Nova. Your sister's name?"

Nova spotted it in the line; it was the card at the end. She picked it up. She wanted to hand it to Francine . . . but how could she? Bridget was not for Francine. Bridget was not for anybody except herself and Nova, same as Nova only existed for herself and Bridget. She could not give Bridget to Francine. If she did, Bridget would not be happy.

Nova could hear her sister's voice in her head.

"If it feels like a home now, it'll just be harder when we have to leave later."

Nova never knew when later would be. Maybe soon. Maybe even tomorrow, when Mrs. Steele came to do her wellness check.

Nova hugged BRIDGET to her chest. The tips of her ears tingled as she began to shake. Not bounce, not flap, but shake. Billy could put down the camcorder. Francine could put away the cards. They could both go away and leave Nova alone. She did not want any more testing. She did not want any more talking. She did not want any more pretend-to-be-forever family.

Bridget was gone.

And Nova was shaking.

She shook her head one-two-three-four times, hit her temple with her palm one-two-three-four times, bit the space between her thumb and forefinger, and rocked and hummed and flapped, but nothing made her feel better.

She put her forehead on the table and closed her eyes.

"Nova?" asked Francine softly. Billy patted her shoulder. She ignored them.

She was All Done.

3

JAN 25, 1986

Dear Bridget,

T-minus three days until *Challenger* launch.

I have been writing to you every single day.

Have you been writing to me?

Today Francine wanted me to read with her. She made flash cards. They were like the flash cards you made for me in kindergarten except these had no pictures on the back. I think I should be happy because she said she was happy, but I feel not happy. Even though I know my ABCs, reading is hard and writing is harder and I'm afraid I'll never be able to do it like you do. I've always hated how *X* makes a *Z* sound and *C* makes an *S* sound. I also hate how *b* and *p* and *d* and *q* all look kind of the same but are not the same. And I really hated how when you told me "Lowercase *A* is just a moon with a tail!" I could not get my tail to attach to my moon.

I am sorry I hit you when you said try again. I did not want to try again but it was not nice to hit you. At school Mrs. Pierce says "Happy Hands" means no hitting. She says hitting is very bad. She says after we hit, we say sorry. So I am also sorry I did not say sorry after I hit you, Bridget.

And I am extra sorry because I hit Bouncing Buddy at school yesterday.

It happened at Morning Circle. I was trying to make Music Margot's head stay up when Miss Chambers made me switch seats with Bouncing Buddy. This put me next to Wispy Lip Luke and him next to Bossy Mallory.

During the Pledge of Allegiance, Buddy stopped bouncing and snatched Mallory's glasses right off her face.

"Give them back, Buddy!" she shouted. He put them on his own face. She screamed louder, "Give them back!"

He ran away from Circle and jumped up on my desk. He was laughing. Mallory started to cry, which is different because Quiet Mary-Beth is usually the one who cries. Mallory says crying is for babies.

Mrs. Pierce asked Buddy two times very nicely to give them back but he did not so I climbed up on the table too and punched him in the shoulder. Then I took back Mallory's glasses and brought them to her. Buddy climbed down and went back to his seat.

Mallory was happy and I was happy but Miss Chambers was not happy. She said, "Happy Hands means no hitting, Nova! Hitting our friends is never allowed!"

After school when Francine came, Mrs. Pierce told her about what I did.

On the drive home, Francine said she was "very disappointed" in me.

NASA Bear felt very disappointed too.

Am I turning into a bad girl? One who burns cookies, hits friends, and does not try hard at testing?

Tomorrow Mrs. Steele will come.

I want Billy and Francine to tell her good things, not like the last foster family who always told her bad things.

I want them to say I can stay.

I want them to let you stay too.

I want you and the Wests together to be my forever family.

I want you to be proud of me.

The *Challenger* launches in three days, Bridget.

I will be waiting for you at Jefferson Middle School in Mr. O'Reilly's classroom on the first floor, sixth-grade wing, room 106, past the *Bridge to Terabithia* poster.

I know you will find me because you found me before, and also because you promised.

But every day I'm a little more worried.

I miss you.

Love,
Your Super Nova

Chapter Nine

Joanie woke Nova up early on Sunday morning.

"Get dressed," she whispered. "We're going to breakfast at the diner, just us!"

Nova hopped out of bed. She loved the diner. They had silver dollar pancakes with whipped butter and pecan syrup at the diner. She rushed to the bathroom and returned with her teeth brushed and face washed. She pulled on her favorite Olive Green overalls, which Joanie fastened, over a long-sleeved Brick-Red-and-Maize-striped shirt, with Cornflower blue slouch socks. Joanie fixed her hair and tried to give her a hug, but Nova wriggled away. She liked Joanie and she liked the diner, but she still did not like hugging. . . . Not much, anyway.

"Come on, let's go! We have to be back before Mrs. Steele gets here."

Nova frowned. In her the excitement over the diner, she'd forgotten about the social worker. Knowing Mrs. Steele would soon be in the house suddenly had Nova's stomach all in knots, knots like the ones in her shoelaces she could never untangle. Even though she'd seen Mrs. Steele every single month for the past five years, she could not help fearing each visit. This was mostly because she never knew ahead of time if it was going to be a check or a removal. But once they got to the diner she didn't want to ruin breakfast, so like Peter Pan she tried to "think happy thoughts."

Joanie insisted Nova order her own food by pointing to pictures on the menu. Nova chose the silver dollar pancakes, of course, with a side of bacon, and doused both with pecan syrup. Joanie ordered eggs and corned beef hash with toast and they drank Coke from glass bottles. While they ate, Joanie talked and talked and talked. Nova tried to listen, but she was distracted by the sights and sounds in the diner, which was already bustling even though it was only nine-thirty, which meant church hadn't let out yet (there was always a line at the door once church let out). She smiled, though, and said "Mm" every so often, and Joanie seemed happy because she kept smiling too.

On the drive back, Joanie pulled over. She turned down the music—she'd been singing along to "Let's Dance" by David Bowie, while Nova, in the front seat beside her, was tapping her hands on her knees to the beat—and put the car in park.

"That song had me thinking," said Joanie. She pointed to something on the side of the road. "See the cross on the embankment, Nova?"

It was painted white, made of wood, stuck in the mud.

"I know you've ridden by it before, with Mom."

"Mm," said Nova. Yes, Francine had pointed it out before, but Nova wasn't sure she was supposed to care. A cross was nothing but painted wood stuck in the ground. She did not look at the cross. She was ready to be All Done with this talk now.

"The cross reminds us that . . . that we . . ." Joanie paused, searching for words. "We miss people when they're gone, but we keep them with us by remembering them. Even if they're *not* passed, but, like, gone for some reason, we miss them and remember them—like how I miss my brothers because they all grew up and moved away. I keep a picture of them in my room, and when I look at it I remember all the time I spent following them around when I was younger, before they went to college. Like how I'm leaving to go back to college tomorrow. Which is why we went to the diner. You know?"

Joanie wasn't making much sense, in Nova's opinion, so Nova did *not* know. But she said "Mm" because she was ready to be All Done.

Joanie was not All Done.

"And that's okay! It's okay for you to miss your mom, and it's okay for me to miss my brothers, like how I know you miss Bridget . . ."

Nova tilted her head slightly. Missing someone was what you did when they were away, when they were gone. She remembered Bridget telling her that when they were first taken away from Mama.

"I know you miss Mama," Bridget used to say. "I miss her too."

But Nova *didn't* miss Mama. Not anymore. She could hardly remember her, and what she did remember was just okay. They baked one time and that was fun, and they would walk down to the brook to skip stones sometimes, but she didn't know what to expect with Mama. Not like Bridget.

"So, like, what I'm trying to say . . ."

"Mm!" Nova wanted to tell her to just spit it out already.

"I guess my point is that family is . . . there are a lot of different kinds of families, you know?"

"Mm," said Nova. She couldn't help feeling like she was overusing that word today, but this time, she *did* know. Their first foster mother read them a book about *All Kinds of Families*.

"Some kids live with two parents, some live with grandparents, some have lots of brothers, some have just one sister, and some are only children. You see?"

Nova did *not* see how this family stuff had anything to do with sitting here by a cross on the side of the road *or* with the diner *or* with college *or* with David Bowie on the radio.

"In some families, everyone looks alike. Like my two oldest brothers. People used to think they were twins! But sometimes family members look *really* different, like my mom and me, with different skin color, different hair texture, different eyes . . . you know? And that's okay."

"Mm?" Nova bounced in her seat and tap-tap-tapped the radio dial. More music, not more silly talk about families having different eyes. She couldn't even remember Bridget's eyes.

"Also, it's okay to miss someone we love when they're not with us, but it's okay to learn to love new people too." Joanie reached across the middle seat like she was going to hold Nova's tapping hand, but Nova pulled it back and dug her fingers into NASA Bear's fur so Joanie's hand retreated to the steering wheel. "I know you miss Bridget and want her to come back, and you miss your mom and probably want her back too, but I also know that my parents adore you, and I do too, so . . . what if we could be your family? That'd be nice, wouldn't it?"

This time, Nova didn't say "Mm." She stared at Joanie's dark purple fingernails on the steering wheel and thought about how Bridget used to paint hers too. Neon green was her favorite. She sometimes tried to do

Nova's to match, but Nova couldn't sit still long enough for them to dry so polish would end up on her clothes and fuzz would end up on her nails.

Joanie continued. "Bridget will always be your big sister like my big brothers will always be my big brothers, but maybe we could be sisters too. You and me. Like a forever family. You know?"

Nova didn't know the answer to that one. She had never wanted any other sisters. Just Bridget. Bridget and Nova. Like Beezus and Ramona. But she had *fun* with Joanie. She *wanted* to stay with the Wests. She liked the *idea* of a forever family.

"Like I said, I'm going back to college tomorrow." This time Joanie did reach out and touch her hand, but only for a second. "I'll miss you, but I'll be home again for Easter. You'll meet my brothers then too. And their wives. And my nephews! They're the cutest. They'll love you! Mom says you know a lot of words, like *moon* and *cat,* so maybe we can write letters while I'm gone? And I'll leave you a picture of me and take a picture of you with me. Wouldn't that be nice?"

Nova nodded thoughtfully. It *would* be nice . . . but what would Bridget say?

"My family's been sort of empty since my brothers all went to college and moved far away. But when Mom and Dad brought you home, I don't know, the house started to feel more . . . complete. I like it. I like having a little sister . . ." Joanie picked up NASA Bear and kissed his bubble helmet. "And I like having an astronaut teddy in the house too."

"Na-ah," said Nova, pointing to the word on his chest. "Na-ah Beah."

"NASA Bear?" asked Joanie. "Is that his name?"

Nova squeaked and grinned, bouncing in her seat. She touched the logo on his uniform again.

"Na-ah Beah! Ah! Mm! Na-ah Beah!"

"NASA Bear," repeated Joanie, grinning back. She sat him in the middle seat and shook his furry paw. "Welcome to the family, NASA Bear."

When they pulled into the driveway a few minutes later, a familiar wood-paneled station wagon was parked off to one side. Mrs. Steele had arrived. The knot in Nova's tummy returned, the one she'd had when writing to Bridget yesterday and had again in the morning before the diner. It threatened to make the pecan syrup pancakes come back up, so she swallowed several times, but that didn't help.

"Come on," said Joanie, taking Nova's hand. They entered through the kitchen and continued to the dining room, where Francine was setting out small triangular crustless cucumber sandwiches.

Down the hall, by the front door, Billy was hanging Mrs. Steele's coat in the closet.

"Oh, good, girls, you're just in time!"

Joanie said a quick hello before excusing herself to pack for school. Nova hugged NASA Bear to her chest and glared at Mrs. Steele.

"Back to college already," Billy sighed. "Winter break always passes too fast."

"I know what you mean. I have two in college myself." Mrs. Steele chuckled. "They forget I exist until they run out of money. Hello, Nova."

Nova did not respond.

"Nova," prompted Francine, joining them in the hall. "Say hello to Mrs. Steele."

"It's fine," said Mrs. Steele pleasantly. "She doesn't really understand what we're saying." She waved her hand in an exaggerated way and added, "It Is Lovely To See You Looking Well, Nova!"

"She understands plenty!" insisted Francine. "And there's no need to shout; her hearing is fine. Nova, say hello, please."

The way she said please didn't sound like *please*. It sounded like *now*.

"Hi." Nova waved. The right way, palm out.

"She says hi now! Isn't that darling?"

Mrs. Steele sounded genuinely delighted, which annoyed Nova almost as much as the word *darling*. The adults filed back into the dining room and, with nothing better to do, Nova trailed after them, still fighting to keep her pancakes down.

"Nova is doing very well here," said Billy as Mrs. Steele set her briefcase on the dining room table. "So let's get right to it. We love having her and would like her to stay."

Relieved to hear this, Nova exhaled loudly. So loudly Mrs. Steele jolted.

"All right there, Nova?" she asked, her too-thin eyebrows drawn together.

"Won't you try a sandwich, or perhaps some coffee?" Francine sat across from Mrs. Steele. Billy settled to her left, with a seat in between them for Nova. He tapped the back of the chair. With a small sigh, Nova sat. She glanced around the room. She hadn't spent much time in here, since they always ate in the kitchen. Like the downstairs parlor, the dining room was fancy and formal and dull. The wallpaper was white with off-white accents. The wood floors were dark and shiny. The oak table could easily seat ten. There was even a small piano between the two long windows that faced the backyard pool, though the view was hidden behind heavy velvet drapes. She much preferred the attic.

Mrs. Steele removed a thick manila folder full of papers, a yellow notepad, and two pens, one black, one blue, from her briefcase.

Though Nova disliked the texture of cucumbers and was still feeling sort of sick, she picked up one of the crustless sandwiches and began to munch. She set NASA

Bear on the table in front of her so she had a free hand to tap her chin while she chewed.

Mrs. Steele looked Nova up and down before jotting something in her notepad.

"I must say, she looks healthy. So much better than she did the last time I saw her."

Francine and Billy exchanged a glance. Nova almost missed it, but at that moment she happened to be checking their faces for any sign that she could head up to her room. She furrowed her brow. Why were they looking at each other that way?

"Nova's back in school now," said Francine.

"After considerable discussion, it was determined she should repeat sixth grade," added Billy.

"Yes, I think that was a good decision," said Mrs. Steele.

"Do you mind if we put this on?" asked Francine, leaning back toward the small fan on the hutch. "It gets so stuffy in here otherwise, with the heat turned up."

"By all means," said Mrs. Steele, who was adding cream to her coffee. It dripped on the table. Billy reached for a napkin.

Nova grunted as the oscillating fan wafted the scent of Aqua Net hairspray from Mrs. Steele's head to Nova's nose. She hated that smell. Bridget used a lot of it too, when trying to tease her hair up huge and wild before parties. Nova hated it when Bridget teased her hair and sprayed Aqua Net because it meant she'd be going out with friends, leaving Nova behind.

Nova imagined Mrs. Steele dressed the way Bridget used to, in a leopard-print top and a black leather skirt, with a dozen thick plastic neon-colored bangle bracelets, torn-up tights, and silver hoop earrings so big they touched her shoulders. Bridget always looked cool, like she could rock out with Madonna, but Mrs. Steele? Ridiculous!

Unable to get this picture out of her head, Nova let out a high screech, followed by three gasping yelps.

Mrs. Steele blanched. "Oh my God, is she choking?"

"That's her laugh!" Francine stared at Mrs. Steele. "You've been her social worker for five *years*. Haven't you heard her laugh before?"

"Goodness, no, I haven't."

Embarrassed, Nova smacked herself one-two-three-four times in the temple, mentally scolding herself for making so much noise. Gently, Billy moved her hand down, giving it a comforting squeeze.

"Sit with us for a few more minutes. Then you can head upstairs, okay?"

She didn't respond, but she did keep sitting. Francine sipped her coffee. Billy ate a sandwich. Mrs. Steele took notes while they talked. Nova stopped listening. Adult conversation was rarely worth listening to. She hummed and rocked as the tension left her body. Billy said they wanted to keep her. Besides, if Mrs. Steele had been planning to remove her today, it would have happened already. She could relax a little.

Now she just had to figure out how to tell Bridget where to find her without knowing where to send her letters. Maybe Mrs. Steele could give her the address. Nova wished she could talk so she could ask the Wests to let Bridget live with them, or ask Mrs. Steele to bring Nova to her for a visit. When they first went into foster care, they used to visit Mama sometimes. If Nova could visit Mama, why couldn't she visit Bridget?

". . . reevaluated at some point within the next year . . . ," Mrs. Steele was saying. "And that will be considered along with the results of her teacher's testing . . ."

Nova shut her eyes and pictured herself from a distance. She was wearing a white astronaut's suit with NASA stamped in blue across the right breast pocket. She was standing on the moon, staring out at the stars. She was alone. Where was Bridget?

Bridget was gone.

And Nova was angry.

Nova was angry because Bridget was gone.

She imagined herself stomping her feet in the moon dust, punching her fists against her own thighs, looking left and right for her missing sister. Bridget had to be there too. She had to! Nova certainly couldn't have flown all the way to the moon alone.

"Tell me, Mrs. West, how *is* Nova doing in school?"

Nova played David Bowie's "Space Oddity" over and over and over again in her head to block out the angry thoughts, to push away the sight of her standing alone with Earth barely visible in the distance. She did not like feeling angry, especially not with Bridget. It was not fair. Bridget almost never got angry with her, not even when Nova was hitting.

Every now and then, a bit of what Mrs. Steele or Billy or Francine was saying would force its way into her brain, but mostly Nova could tune them out, wrapped up in her own world, far away, and safe.

"*. . . floating in a most peculiar way . . .*"

". . . think she can read! She was able to identify several words and most of her letters. Not one hundred percent of the time but enough that it couldn't be a fluke . . ."

"*. . . stars look very different today . . .*"

". . . lovely that you're so supportive, but remember, Nova is an autistic, cognitively impaired child. You can only expect so much . . ."

"*. . . sitting in a tin can . . .*"

". . . we have faith that a good school and a stable, loving family will make all the difference in the world . . ."

"*. . . far above the world . . .*"

". . . if you're sure you understand what such a commitment would entail . . ."

"*. . . planet Earth is blue . . .*"

"Yes, we understand."

Suddenly they were standing. Nova jumped up too. The song stopped. The moon evaporated into space dust. She was all ready to say goodbye to Mrs. Steele but instead of heading to the coat closet by the front door, the three adults headed to the parlor, cups of coffee in hand.

Nova grabbed NASA Bear and grunted.

"You can go upstairs and play," said Billy. "Or watch TV. The remote's on top."

Nova did not know how to use the remote control, which was square, had too many buttons, and weighed as much as an actual brick, but she was eager to escape the conversation. She had made it halfway up the front stairs, which led to the landing outside the master bedroom on the opposite side of the house from her room, when Francine's words halted her.

". . . don't know what she understands about Bridget."

"I tried to explain it," said Mrs. Steele. "Those first few days I was with Nova constantly. I felt she might be looking for Bridget, and I did my best to make her understand. But like I keep telling you, though she's a nice girl, she simply *cannot* comprehend *most* of what we say. Why keep explaining what she's never going to get?"

"We don't agree," said Billy. "We think she's much smarter than you realize."

Nova smiled. She was nice. She was smart. This was good. She sat on the step to listen some more.

"Do we know why the girls tried to run away?" asked Francine. "Were they being neglected?"

"No, nothing like that. I've completed an investigation of the family. They have four other foster daughters, all perfectly fine. The mother blamed that boyfriend . . ."

Nova cocked her head to one side. What boyfriend? Who had a boyfriend? Nova certainly did not have a boyfriend.

"You think he was a bad influence?" asked Billy.

"How did Bridget meet him?" asked Francine.

Oh, Bridget, remembered Nova. *That's right,* Bridget *had a boyfriend. The boy who drove the car, dressed like a vampire, and held her hand at the movies. That* boyfriend.

"Through friends. After a while, she was failing two of her classes, which should have been a red flag."

"Because . . . ?"

"Because despite everything that happened after their father was killed in Vietnam, even with their mother's issues and eventual death, despite moving around from family to family and changing schools multiple times, and even with . . . even with having Nova around like her *shadow,* Bridget was always an honor roll student."

Nova was suddenly presented with the mental image of Bridget as Peter Pan, trying to stick Nova, her shadow, back on with soap, the way it happened in the story. She liked that thought, that they would always be attached to each other, and didn't understand why Mrs. Steele said "shadow" like it was bad. Peter Pan loved his shadow. Who didn't love their shadow?

"Their previous foster parents told me during a wellness check a few months ago that they weren't happy about Bridget's grades and behavior, but with more pressing things to worry about . . ."

"You're telling us she fell through the cracks?" asked Francine, her voice rising. Nova sat on the carpeted stairs and pressed NASA Bear's furry belly against her face, inhaling his scent, a mix of musk and laundry detergent.

"I hate to say 'fell through the cracks . . .'"

"But she did! Like her mother, and Nova too. As my husband said, she's far more capable than she's given credit for. If only she'd had proper special education from the beginning, if she'd had consistency, if she'd stayed in one place long enough to—"

"I'm sorry," interrupted Mrs. Steele, sounding not-sorry, "but we have a lot of kids in terrible situations." She huffed indignantly. "I regret what happened with Bridget, but considering all the kids on my caseload, I couldn't devote a lot of extra resources toward a girl whose primary offenses were talking back, slipping grades, and coming home late for dinner—in other words, a typical teen!"

"But she—" Billy started. Mrs. Steele cut him off.

"She was acting like every other girl her age! To be perfectly honest, when she started dressing up, going out, taking life a little less seriously, I thought, *Great! This will be good for her!* When I first met the Vezina girls, Bridget was twelve. She was the most serious and responsible seventh grader I'd ever seen, an academic overachiever, determined to change the world. She was practically raising her sister, she had few friends, and I rarely saw her smile. She had many good qualities, don't get me wrong, but she was such a stressed-out little girl! She once called me crying because she earned a C on a science quiz and wanted to be moved to a new family so she could attend a different school before some big test. I had to tell her we don't recommend removal for reasons like that and suggested she just keep studying. Two weeks later, she called to tell me she'd earned an A on the exam, highest score in the class. She said she didn't expect praise, she just thought I should know."

"She sounds just like Joanie," said Billy. "Joanie's grades were always very important to her too. Anything below a B was a disaster."

Nova smiled. If Bridget was "just like Joanie," maybe Bridget and Joanie would like being sisters. A forever family. With Nova, Billy, and Francine.

And NASA Bear, of course.

"I'm not sure *what* Bridget was thinking when she ran away, nor can I say why she took Nova with her," said Mrs. Steele, her voice wavering. "It was uncharacteristically irresponsible. I'm just glad . . ."

"You're glad she's with us now," Francine said. "So are we."

Mrs. Steele changed the subject to paperwork. Several minutes went by with no more mention of Bridget, so Nova continued upstairs, down the hall, past the TV room, and into her bedroom, where she stopped only long enough to grab Bridget's Walkman and the tape before heading up to the attic. Thoughts were falling through her brain faster than shooting stars in the planetarium.

She was going to stay with the Wests.

For now.

But Bridget was *still* gone.

And Nova was confused.

She rested on her knees facing the round attic window and slipped the headphones over her ears. She hit Rewind and rocked back and forth while she waited for the click signaling that the tape had reached the beginning. She pressed Play. David Bowie filled her ears. Rocking back and forth, she could almost hear Bridget singing along.

Goose bumps trickled up her arms.

Bridget had sung "Space Oddity" to Nova so many times they felt like they'd written it, like it was theirs and theirs alone, not to be shared with the rest of the world.

"Ground Control to Major Tom . . ."

2

JAN 26, 1986

Dear Bridget,

T-minus two days until *Challenger* launch.

Mrs. Steele came today. She talked to Billy and Francine. She told them about your boyfriend and running away and the bad grades you were getting.

Francine said you fell through a crack and I fell through a crack and even Mama fell through a crack and she sounded mad about it.

I don't know what crack she's talking about.

I know it's not okay to step on a crack. Mama used to say that.

"Don't step on a crack or you'll break your mother's back!"

I remember one time Mama was walking me to the store and I did step on a crack and then I cried and cried and cried because I thought her back was broken, but she picked me up and laughed and laughed and carried me the rest of the way so I guess it didn't hurt too bad.

Billy thinks your boyfriend was a bad influence. I do not know what *influence* means, but I thought he was bad too. I know you liked him, but I did not. He sang too loud and drove too fast and he was always taking you away from me.

I was mad at you the day I met him, Bridget.

I was mad at you even though it was your birthday.

I was mad because we were supposed to go straight to Sugarbaker's Sweets Shoppe to get ice cream cones with rainbow sprinkles, but you took us to that boy's house instead.

I was mad because you said "I'll be quick!" but you were not quick.

I was mad because I could hear you talking to him and laughing with him and kissing on him while I was supposed to be watching TV.

I did not want to watch TV.

I was mad about that too. I was mad because I had to sit and watch the news when I was supposed to be eating rainbow sprinkles.

By the time the boy's sister got home and all four of us were in the car, I didn't even want ice cream anymore. I felt too sick in my stomach. I made a lot of noise because I wanted you to know I wanted to go home, but you buckled my seat belt and promised me rainbow sprinkles and asked me to "Pretty, pretty please, with a cherry on top, just be good."

You handed me NASA Bear.

And it was your birthday.

So I tried to just be good.

But I know I was not that good. I know it was not good to accidentally step on his foot while we waited for a booth. I know it was not good to accidentally dip NASA Bear's paw in his banana split. I know it was not good to accidentally throw my cherry at him . . . twice.

I did not try too hard to just be good.

I am sorry I did not try.

Before Mrs. Steele came today, Joanie took me to the diner. Just us. I was very good.

On the way back, we stopped by a cross on the side of the road. Joanie got sad but I don't know why. She said it's okay to miss someone we love when they're not with us, but I already knew that. You told me the same thing a long time ago. You said it was okay to miss Mama but she was too sick to take care of us. Then, after the visits stopped, you said she went to Asteroid B-612 to "rake out her active volcanoes," like the Little Prince in our book.

You said I should be happy because Mama wouldn't feel sick in space.

You said she wasn't coming back.

Tomorrow, Joanie will leave for college. But she will come back for Easter.

Bridget, tell me the truth.

Where is Mama?

You told me she went to space to feel better, but people come back from space. Like Buzz Aldrin. And Sally Ride. And Valentina Tereshkova.

Is Mama with the Little Prince, like you said?

Where are you?

I miss you.

> Love,
> Your Super Nova

Chapter Ten

On Monday, Nova awoke extra early again, but instead of slipping up to the attic she sat on the floor beside the wooden crate with JOANIE ROSE painted on it and pulled out her toys. She hadn't touched most of them since the last time she'd played with Bridget because they used to play together and Nova wasn't sure she could figure out pretending on her own. Bridget was always the one who came up with the ideas for their games, the one who assigned roles and decided what would happen to their little astronauts or aliens.

Even though she wasn't as good at imagining as Bridget was, Nova needed to pretend. She needed to feel the way she felt when they'd play pretend.

Mostly, they played alone. But for the months they lived in the temporary home with the seven other kids, Bridget let everybody join. Nova had just turned ten.

Bridget was almost fifteen. They were exploring in the woods behind the horse pasture when they found the tree house.

"It's perfect, Nova!" Bridget shouted from inside. Nova was on the ground, too cautious to climb. "This can be our space station!"

They returned to the house to gather the other kids. Four of them were in foster care too, but the twins and the toddler were the family's biological kids.

"I'll set the scene," said Bridget, once everyone was gathered at the base of the tree house. "It's 1969." She pointed at the twins. "You two are Ground Control in Houston. Me, Nova, Suzanne, and Anthony are headed to the moon. You two"—she pointed to the oldest two, who were eleven and twelve—"are President Nixon and First Lady Pat, watching from the White House Communications Room."

"What 'bout me?" asked the toddler, who was still in diapers.

"You? You're . . . um . . . you're very important! You're in charge of . . . um . . . you're . . . why, you're the Nixons' dog, of course! Checkers! Good dog, Checkers."

The toddler barked. Bridget patted his head. He was a good dog.

"Okay," she said. "I'm Buzz Aldrin. Nova, you're Neil Armstrong, first man to set foot on the moon. Anthony, you're Michael Collins, the one who stayed on the spacecraft. And Suzanne, you're . . . um . . . Sally Ride."

"What?" Suzanne put her hands on her hips. "Sally Ride wasn't on the moon mission. She just went to space last month!"

"It's pretend! Geez!" Bridget let out a frustrated puff of air. She hated it when anyone questioned her during Space Play. "Wanna play Checkers's groomer instead? No? Then be Sally Ride. This tree house is Apollo 11. Armstrong? Collins? Ride? Up here."

Bridget scrambled about two-thirds of the way up the tree house ladder, which was really a bunch of uneven boards nailed into the tree. Nova followed slowly, cautiously, clinging to the trunk, afraid to fall even though it was only a couple of feet to the ground. Collins and Ride hopped on the ladder after her, though Ride muttered something about "Bossy Bridget."

"Okay, Ground Control? It's your job to help get us in the air. President Nixon, take your wife and dog over there. You'll be waiting for confirmation once we make it out of Earth's atmosphere. President Kennedy, before he died, swore we'd make it to the moon before the decade's end. It's already the middle of 1969. We're running out of time. Let's show those Russian cosmonauts who's winning the space race! Let's do it for President Kennedy!"

"For Kennedy!" shouted the Ground Control twins, pumping their fists in the air.

"It's nine-thirty a.m." Bridget pretended to check her watch. "T-minus two minutes."

Nova's tummy fluttered. She knew it was pretend but at the same time it felt so real. She blinked as the forest around them faded. In two minutes she knew she would be soaring above the clouds and into the dark abyss of the universe beyond tiny planet Earth. She was scared but excited.

"Ten, nine, eight . . ."

Everyone except Nova and Checkers the dog counted down.

"Seven, six, five . . ."

Bridget nudged Nova. She wanted her to count too.

Nova tried.

"Foh, tee, two, uhn . . ."

Lift-off!

The four on the ladder scrambled up to their space shuttle tree house. It had two rooms. The room in front, where the ladder led, had a balcony railing attached from one tree branch to another. Sally Ride and Nova held on to it, watching the stars slip by on either side, while Collins and Bridget-as-Buzz moved to the back room, pretending to mess with controls.

"Success!" shouted Bridget. "A perfect launch!"

"They made it!" President Nixon hugged his wife. "We're going to the moon, Pat! Ahead of those Soviets. Eat our space dust!"

"I don't think President Nixon would say 'Eat our

space dust,'" snickered one of the Ground Control Twins. The others laughed too, but not Bridget or Nova, because space is serious business.

"No fooling around!" Bridget ordered. "That's how mistakes are made."

The Ground Control Twins turned back to their controls, adjusting acorn knobs, pretending to speak to the shuttle through a pinecone.

"Apollo 11, this is Ground Control. What's your status?"

Bridget-as-Buzz spoke into her own pinecone. "Ground Control, it's been three days and we're now in lunar orbit. All systems still go? We good for a soft landing on the moon? Has to be a soft landing. A hard landing could destroy the craft and kill us all."

"Sure thing," answered a Ground Control Twin. "Bring her down."

"Collins, steer us manually," Bridget-as-Buzz ordered. "Over these boulders into the Sea of Tranquility."

"We're landing in a sea?" asked Sally Ride, clutching the handrail so hard her knuckles had gone white. Maybe she was motion-sick. Or afraid of heights. Nova wished she could tell her it was okay. Bridget *always* managed a soft landing.

"It's not a real sea, right?" asked President Nixon. "That's what Armstrong named it after they landed."

"Right," confirmed Bridget-as-Buzz. "There's no water on the moon, not that we've ever found, anyway."

"Oh," said Sally Ride.

"We only have thirty seconds of fuel left," said Bridget-as-Buzz. Nova closed her eyes and braced for impact.

"We did it!"

Nova opened her eyes, relieved. Even though she trusted Bridget, the landing always made her nervous.

"Armstrong, tell Ground Control, 'The Eagle has landed.'" Bridget lowered her voice. "Nova, that's you . . . Say 'The Eagle has landed.'"

"Uh Ego ah lah-dah."

Ground Control and the Nixons applauded. Checkers barked, wagging his tail.

"Take the flag," Bridget-as-Buzz said, thrusting some leaves attached to a long, skinny twig into Nova's hand. "Go plant it down there on the surface and say, 'That's one small step for a man, one giant leap for mankind.'"

Cautiously, Nova-as-Armstrong made her way down the ladder to the moon's dusty white surface. She planted the flag in the ground, making sure it was standing up straight.

"Uh mah tep," she said proudly.

President Nixon saluted.

Nova-as-Armstrong was making her way back up the ladder serenaded by cheers and happy barks from the crowd below when a sickening creak stabbed her through the stomach. She stopped breathing.

The rotting wood floor of the back room of the tree house was giving way. The boy playing Collins leapt forward into the first room, but Bridget didn't have time to grab for the railing or even one of the nearby branches. She fell hard through the rotted wood and landed on her elbow. When she stood up, her arm was bent the wrong way. Backward.

"Mission accomplished," she announced, grinning. She looked down at her floppy busted arm, then at the flag Nova-as-Armstrong had planted on the moon's surface.

She didn't even cry.

After she got her cast, she let Nova be the first to draw on it.

Nova drew the moon, because they'd made it.

When Bridget was in charge, they always made it.

With Bridget gone, Nova would have to try to make it on her own.

She had one hour before it was time to get ready for school.

One hour.

In the wooden crate labeled JOANIE ROSE there were several old toys: a Mr. Potato Head (with all his random plastic body parts), a dozen brightly colored Matchbox cars, a one-armed G.I. Joe in a yellow helicopter, a Barbie doll in a sparkly pink gown, a second Barbie with long black hair and a Hawaiian print dress, a Rubik's Cube, a Magic 8 Ball, several beat-up-looking board games, two yo-yos, half of a walkie-talkie set, a Luke

Skywalker action figure with a broken lightsaber, and a plastic Princess Leia all in white.

Nova smiled. She was not a *Star Wars* fan, but Princess Leia could easily play a payload specialist. Luke Skywalker, the Barbies, and G.I. Joe could be other astronauts. The walkie-talkie would be a perfect tool for communicating with NASA Bear, who always played Ground Control when they didn't have enough kids.

Nova stuffed Luke and Leia inside the chopper. It was too small to fit the other astronauts so the Barbies and G.I. Joe watched from on top of the toy box.

Nova began a countdown in her head.

Ten, nine, eight, seven . . .

Ground Control, thought Nova, pressing the walkie-talkie to her lips. *Come in, Ground Control. We're ready for lift-off. Over.*

Take your protein pills and put your helmet on, answered Ground Control NASA Bear.

Nova moved Princess Leia so it looked like she was nodding.

. . . *six, five, four* . . .

It would be easier with music, Nova decided. Less lonely. She scurried over to the bedside table and pulled Bridget's Walkman from the drawer. She slipped the headphones over her ears and pressed Play.

David Bowie filled her head. The song was half over, but she didn't bother to rewind.

. . . three, two, one, lift-off!

Princess Leia and Luke Skywalker rocketed into space on G.I. Joe's yellow helicopter/space shuttle. On the floor, Ground Control watched and waited, his furry fingers crossed.

Nova held her breath . . . just a little farther . . .

Soaring *"past one hundred thousand miles . . ."*

Yes!

She made it! She made it into outer space!

Nova stood, holding the helicopter/space shuttle high, zooming it around the room past furniture and stars. Back on Earth, NASA Bear and G.I. Joe and the Barbies applauded.

Success!

". . . floating 'round my tin can, far above the moon . . ."

Fast approaching, ready to land! It would need to be a soft landing. A hard landing on the moon could damage the craft and injure the astronauts. It had to be perfect. No room for error.

Nova scrambled up onto the bed, reaching the helicopter/space shuttle toward the hanging white globe that covered the light in the center of the room. She stretched her arm, stretched her spine. She could almost reach it. She could almost reach the moon. Just a little closer . . .

A loud thump on the door surprised Nova. She lost her balance, waving her arms to keep from falling off the bed. She managed to plop backward onto her pillow, but the helicopter/space shuttle was not so lucky. It flew from her hand, smashed against the edge of the dresser, and dropped to the floor. The propeller was broken.

Oh, no, said NASA Bear from his position at Ground Control. *Houston, we've had a problem.*

Nova screamed. The shuttle was broken. Luke Skywalker was on the floor. Princess Leia was nowhere in sight.

The bedroom door opened.

"Nova, I've been knocking. Are you okay?" Joanie rushed to her side. She took off the headphones, checked Nova over, and even felt her head like she might have a fever. Nova pulled away. She returned the Walkman to the bedside table drawer, wiping her eyes, shaking. The song had ended anyway. The game was over.

"Mom sent me up to tell you it's time to get ready for school," said Joanie, trying to smile. "Don't worry about the toys; you can clean up later. I'm glad you were playing." She picked up Hawaiian Barbie and smoothed down her dress. "I loved these dolls when I was your age! This one was my favorite. Isn't she pretty?"

Nova did not answer, not even an "Mm."

"So, what do you want to wear today?" Joanie put the doll away and went to the dresser. She held up a red-and-white-striped shirt with long sleeves and a pair of denim overalls. "How about this?"

Nova did not care what she wore. She picked up the broken helicopter. They'd had space travel mishaps and emergencies before, but Bridget always managed to save the day. Even when she broke her arm. They still managed Mission Accomplished. Nova held out the helicopter to show Joanie.

"What's wrong? The propeller came off?" Joanie gave Nova a quick hug. Nova did not pull away. "No big deal! We'll glue it."

But it *was* a big deal.

It was.

1

JAN 27, 1986

Dear Bridget,

T-minus one day until *Challenger* launch.

This morning something so bad happened I do not
know if anything can ever be good again, Bridget. Today,
my space shuttle crashed.

The moon mission started okay. NASA Bear played
Ground Control. I did your job, making sure everyone else
knew what to do. Princess Leia and Luke Skywalker were
my astronauts, Sally Ride and Alan Shepard. We were
almost to the moon when I dropped the space shuttle.
I dropped the space shuttle! And it broke! And I can't find
Princess Leia . . . I mean, Sally Ride . . . anywhere!

At breakfast Joanie tried to talk to me about saying
goodbye and Billy tried to talk to me about cupcakes this
weekend and Francine tried to talk to me about getting
a haircut soon, but I could not listen because my brain
was too busy so I started humming louder and louder and
louder until their words were All Done.

At school, my mind had no room for anything else,
especially not testing.

169

I never thought about it before, but Major Tom gets lost every time we listen to "Space Oddity." Ground Control calls him and calls him and he cannot hear them. Every time.

I wanted to pay attention to Mrs. Pierce. I wanted to, Bridget, but I was lost too. I was lost like Major Tom. And you.

It got worse and worse until I exploded.

I was at my desk.

Someone kept saying "Nova! Nova!" over and over and over again but I could not listen.

I covered my ears.

I did not like the sound of the voice in my ears. I only wanted you singing David Bowie in my ears.

I did not like the sound of Buddy bouncing in his chair at his workstation. I did not like the sound of Mallory drumming her long nails on the desktop. I did not like Alex's chatting, Mary-Beth's whisper, the grunting noise Luke made when he got a math fact wrong, Thomas's stuffy nose, or the squeaky left wheel of Margot's wheelchair.

I did not like the sound of the heat in the vents or the freezing rain outside the window or the eighth-grade lunch bell or the chairs scraping or the footsteps and laughter of the students in the hall heading to the cafeteria.

It was too much. Too much. Too many sounds. Too many people lost.

Mama and Daddy. Princess Leia and Major Tom. You and me.

My blood turned to lava, burning me from the inside to the outside and all over, bubbling up with no way to escape. I could not breathe. It was like there was a crack in my space helmet. My oxygen slipped out. I was choking.

Remember our space helmets? They stayed behind at Mama's house in the space shuttle closet with the white moon balloon and the flashlight and the globe. Why didn't we take them with us? We should have taken them with us.

I started to cry again, like a kindergarten baby.

I needed you.

I needed it to be you and me and NASA Bear, our space shuttle, and the moon.

I put one hand on my ear and my other ear against my shoulder. I hit myself one-two-three-four times in the side of the head but that did not help, I still could not breathe, so I grabbed my throat. I grabbed it and scratched and clawed and tried to get my oxygen back, but with a broken space helmet, there was no air.

Miss Chambers held down my hands. Mrs. Pierce was telling me to breathe.

They did not understand.

I did not need to be held down. I did not need to be told to breathe.

I needed a rescue mission. I needed help from Ground Control.

I heard your voice in my head, telling me I was still on Earth, not on the moon. That was the problem, you said, not my helmet. The problem was, I was still on Earth and needed to escape. So I started the countdown but so many thoughts were all over my mind it was hard to hear the numbers.

Ten, nine, eight . . .

"Even with having Nova around like her *shadow* . . ."

. . . seven, six, five . . .

"NASA Bear? Is that his name?"

. . . four, three, two . . .

"You're glad she's with us now. So are we."

. . . one . . .

"Mrs. Vezina, I need you to calm down. . . ."

Lift-off . . .

You, singing "Space Oddity."

I was floating away, up to the dusty Sea of Tranquility on the moon. I thought you were in the space shuttle next to me, but when I looked again, I was alone.

Where were you, Bridget?

Without you, I am lost in space.

In the car after school, Francine said she was very worried. She said I had a meltdown. She said we need to work on a way for me to control my emotions without hurting myself.

She does not understand. She's never lost a shuttle before.

When we got home, I skipped snack because I had to find Princess Leia. I was scared. I was scared she might be gone forever, Bridget. And I thought, if she's gone forever, you might be gone forever too.

I was still searching when Francine came in.

"This was on the counter with a note from Joanie. She says she'll miss us but she's going to telephone once a week and send letters. Won't that be nice? And she hot-glued the propeller. I guess it got broken this morning?"

In her hands was the helicopter.

I ran over to take it from her, but before I touched it I saw something amazing. Almost as amazing as the planetarium. Inside the helicopter was Princess Leia. I mean, Sally Ride. She must have been in there the whole time!

She wasn't lost after all.

I took her out of the helicopter and hugged her and cried and cried, even though I felt happy, not sad.

I promised I will not lose her again and I mean it because I keep my promises, the same way you keep your promises.

The night we ran away, you promised if we got separated, you'd come back for me. You'd be here to watch the *Challenger* launch together, you said. You would not miss it for all the planets in the solar system.

The *Challenger* launches tomorrow, Bridget.

So where are you?

Not lost in space.

I miss you.

Love,
Your Super Nova

Chapter Eleven

Nova should have been tired, since excitement had kept her awake until nearly four in the morning, but she sprang out of her bed like she'd been sleeping on an ejector seat.

The front page of the paper said LIFT-OFF.

Billy read the article aloud over scrambled eggs and bacon.

"'After several delays due to weather and other issues, the space shuttle *Challenger* is finally scheduled to launch later today . . . in classrooms all across America, eager students will be watching via satellite news network CNN. On day three of the six-day mission, teacher Christa McAuliffe will teach two fifteen-minute lessons from space, though perhaps the bigger lesson is one she has already taught students: to follow their dreams, no matter how far away doing so may take them.'"

Nova shrieked, bouncing in her seat. The newspaper said the same thing Bridget had. *Challenger* taught kids anyone could have a dream! Anyone could reach the stars! If you worked hard and wanted it bad enough, anyone could escape to outer space!

Nova hugged NASA Bear to her chest, too excited to eat. Finally Francine said it was time to put on shoes (Billy tied them) and go.

In the car on the way to school, Francine said she wanted to talk about "the meltdown" some more.

"I'm worried about you," she said. "We need to understand why you had the meltdown so we can avoid that in the future. Do you know what *avoid* means? When you avoid something, you stay away from it, or stop it from happening."

"Mm," said Nova, but she was only half listening because "Space Oddity" was playing in her head and she was imagining herself going up in the *Challenger*.

"Maybe we can practice taking deep breaths when you feel upset? Can you take a deep breath?" Francine inhaled loudly and let the air out slowly, sounding like a balloon with a small hole. She glanced quickly at Nova, then returned her eyes to the road. "You try. Deep breath in, let it out slow."

Nova breathed in quickly and puffed out the air. It was cold enough in the car that she could see her breath.

"Try again," urged Francine. "Deep breath in, let it

out slow. This is what you do when you feel *overwhelmed*, so you *avoid* having a meltdown."

Nova breathed in and out three times fast, annoyed because she wanted to get back to floating around outer space in her head in peace. Either she did it right or Francine gave up because they drove the rest of the way with no talking.

Before Morning Circle, Francine wanted to discuss "the meltdown" again with Mrs. Pierce and Miss Chambers, so Nova found herself alone on the rug with Music Margot, who was sitting in her wheelchair, as usual.

Checking to be sure no one was watching, Nova darted forward.

"Hi."

Margot did not answer with words, but she smiled.

"Heppa?" asked Nova. She meant "Help." Margot did not answer, but she was still smiling, so Nova put her hands on either side of Margot's face and gently repositioned her head until it was straight. She let go, feeling glad to have helped, but Margot's head slumped a little to the left again. Nova narrowed her eyes and tried a second time.

Margot's head didn't stay up the second time either, but she laughed. She laughed with her voice and with her Crayola Cadet Blue eyes. Nova knew it was a laugh because it sounded a lot like her own laugh.

Nova was about to try once more when she thought,

Maybe Margot's head just isn't meant to stay up. Like how Buddy wasn't meant to stay still and Mary-Beth wasn't meant to make the *S* sound and Bridget wasn't meant to stay in foster care with parents who thought she belonged in juvenile detention. So Nova held Margot's hand instead, even though she usually didn't like touching people's hands with her hands.

"Mm-ma-uh?" She wanted to say "Madonna." She wanted to ask Margot about Madonna, since Mrs. Pierce said that was her favorite singer. Madonna had been one of Bridget's favorites too. Maybe Nova could bring in Bridget's tape and they could listen to Madonna together. She held up Margot's hand and tapped their palms together in a high five. Margot's grin grew, but her head slipped forward until her chin was on her chest.

"Nova! Be careful with your friend!" Miss Chambers walked over and gently guided Margot's head back up, then wheeled her to her usual Morning Circle spot. Nova picked a seat between Alex and Mallory but could not stop squirming. She had to be prompted twice to stand for the Pledge and she forgot to keep quiet during the moment of silence. When it was over, they returned to their desks. She was unable to concentrate at all on her testing with Mrs. Pierce. She could not identify letters, not even those in her own name.

"I know you're excited, Nova, but please calm down and try a little harder," said Mrs. Pierce, rubbing her temples like her head was hurting. "Francine told me how well you did with words and letters over the weekend, but if you can't show *me* what you already know, I won't know what to teach you next."

Nova tried her best, but she was too excited and distracted and . . . she thought back to that word Francine used all the time . . . *overwhelmed,* that was it. She felt overwhelmed. So when Mrs. Pierce asked for *N* she handed her *M* and when Mrs. Pierce requested *Q* she got *O* and when she wanted *Z* she got *H,* which didn't look similar at all. Nova started to get agitated and bounced in her chair, making an angry "Mm" sound.

"Maybe you should take a deep breath?" said Mrs. Pierce. "Francine said you did a good job taking deep breaths this morning."

Nova took a deep breath. It didn't help.

Finally it was time to put the flash cards away.

"Class!" said Mrs. Pierce, clapping her hands to get everyone's attention. "Please return to Morning Circle. As you all know, the *Challenger* space shuttle launches today, and as a nice surprise, we have a special guest here to talk to us about it!"

Nova cocked her head to the side, her eyes wide. A nice surprise? A special guest? Could it be Bridget? Wriggling her fingers excitedly, she hurried to the circle and sat in the same seat she'd occupied earlier, beside Alex.

"Maybe is a astronaut," said Alex. "A real-life one!"

"Maybe it's Valentina Cornucopia," said Mallory. "The first woman in space!"

Nova let out her biggest laugh, shaking her head. Mrs. Pierce had read them a book about the first woman in space, a Russian cosmonaut who orbited Earth forty-eight times in 1963, but her name wasn't Valentina *Cornucopia;* it was Valentina *Tereshkova.*

"What?" asked Mallory, her eyes flashing furiously. "What's so funny?"

Nova shook her head again, but she had no way of correcting her friend, so when Mrs. Pierce asked them all to have quiet voices and calm bodies she folded her hands across NASA Bear's tummy and held back her giggles. Mallory must not have stayed mad long, because she shrugged and smiled and took her seat too, right next to Nova.

Once they were all sitting with Quiet Voices, Listening Ears, and Calm Bodies like the list of rules reminded them to, Mrs. Pierce nodded to Miss Chambers, who was standing by the door. Miss Chambers opened it, and Nova, clutching NASA Bear, held her breath.

Bridget?

But the smiling teenage girl who entered was *not* Bridget.

"Class, this is Stephanie! She's a student at the high school, right across campus, where she's studying astronomy and space travel. She would like to work for NASA someday. Would any of you like to work for NASA someday? Raise your hands!"

Nova jumped out of her chair, put both hands in the air, and squeaked. Not Bridget, but she was happy to see Stephanie. Wispy Lip Luke and Mallory had raised their hands too, but just one each.

"Stephanie already knows Nova because they went to the planetarium together last week, but let's introduce ourselves one at a time . . . from our seats." (Miss Chambers motioned for Nova to return to her chair.) "Let's start with you, Buddy. What is your name?"

At the end of the semicircle, Bouncing Buddy touched the center of his chest with an open palm, then made a sort of X with the index and middle fingers of both hands, and finally folded his thumb across his left palm, raised the other four fingers, and waved palm-out.

"He signed, 'My name's Buddy,'" explained Mr. Malone, handing him a piece of gummy worm. Nova felt a surge of jealousy. If she could talk with her hands like Buddy, she could tell Mallory the first woman in space was Valentina *Tereshkova*. Nova sighed. She hugged NASA Bear and imagined him saying, "Don't feel bad, Nova. No one can hear me talk or read my 'scribbles' either."

After the rest of the class had been introduced, Stephanie unfolded a huge piece of black cardboard split into three parts. Mr. Malone helped her prop it up on the

Morning Circle easel. Nova tried her hardest not to squeak and bounce, but it was beautiful. As beautiful as the solar system poster.

In the middle of the center panel, there was a huge glossy cutout of the space shuttle. Beneath it, a color photograph of the seven astronauts. They were wearing their powder-blue uniforms, holding their helmets. Other pictures included the famous photo of the American flag from the moon landing TV broadcast, a shadowed image of Earth as seen from the moon during the Apollo 8 mission, in which the top of the planet was bright blue and green while the bottom was in the dark, and the exact same image of smiling Sally Ride that Bridget used to have saved inside her Trapper Keeper.

On the left panel, in white writing surrounded by dotted stars, Stephanie had listed SPACE TRAVEL FACTS. On the right panel, she'd pasted newspaper clippings, including many of the ones Nova had saved at home, under the heading CHALLENGER LAUNCH FACTS. All words Nova recognized.

"Let's start with some space travel facts!" said Stephanie, grinning. "Does anyone know who was the first human in space and where he was from?"

Nova whimpered. *Not this again!*

"Yuri Gagarin!" shouted Mallory. "Cosmonaut! Russia! We learned that in Mr. O'Reilly's room."

"Very good!" Stephanie handed her a small square

of something pink that looked like hard cotton candy. "Anyone who gets a question right gets some astronaut ice cream. It's freeze-dried, which means all water has been removed by a vacuuming process that lowers the air pressure, turning it from liquid to solid! Don't worry, there's enough for everyone."

Nova shot Mallory a sharp look. It wasn't fair. She wanted the most astronaut ice cream because she knew the most about space!

"Next question! Does anyone know who the first woman in space was?" asked Stephanie.

"Valentina!" shouted Mallory.

Not Cornucopia, thought Nova.

"Cornucopia!" added Mallory.

"Mm," grumbled Nova. She folded her arms across her chest, nearly knocking NASA Bear from her lap.

"So close! It was Valentina Tereshkova, another Russian cosmonaut."

That was not close, thought Nova.

"Let's remember to raise hands," said Mrs. Pierce gently. "And give our friends a turn."

"Can anyone tell me who was the first American in space?" Stephanie gestured toward Alex, whose face had just lit up. "Do you know?"

"Yes!" said Alex. "Name is Alan, almost Alex! We readed it in the book, right, Mrs. Pierce?"

"Read it," corrected Mr. Malone softly.

"Read it in the book," said Alex. "Alan."

"That's right!" Stephanie was beaming. "It was Alan Shepard. And John Glenn was the first to orbit the earth." She handed a small white square to Alex, who ate it right away, unlike Mallory (who was still holding her pink square).

"What about the first American woman in space?" asked Stephanie. "I'll give you a hint. She did it in 1983, and bonus points if you can tell me the name of her spacecraft."

"Ahh!" shouted Nova, jumping from her seat. NASA Bear landed by her feet. "Ahh!"

Without waiting for permission (and before Miss Chambers could tell her to sit back down), she rushed up to Stephanie's board, slapped her right hand against Sally Ride's smiling face, then tapped the cutout of the *Challenger* repeatedly with the first two fingers of her left. "Ahh!" she said over and over. "Ahh, ahh!"

"Well done, Nova! Nova's right! The first American woman in space was Sally Ride, and she went up *twice* on the *Challenger,* the same *Challenger* launching today! You're an expert, Nova. I bet you could teach everybody even more about space than I can!"

"Mm, ahh!" said Nova, clapping her hands together as she turned to face her class. She glanced at the door. She wished Bridget was here to see this, to see her teaching the other kids about space, to see her being an expert.

"Here's your ice cream!"

Nova accepted her soft brown square (chocolate!) and returned to her seat. She let NASA Bear have a nibble first, then popped the rest in her mouth, which momentarily distracted her from the lesson. It was the strangest sensation. It wasn't cold, and yet it was. It melted in her mouth like ice cream but didn't taste like melty ice cream. It was weird and good at the same time.

"Well done, Nova!" exclaimed Miss Chambers, squeezing her shoulders. "That was wonderful, the way you gave the answer! So smart!" Her face was pink.

Nova did not like the shoulder squeeze much, but she did like being "so smart." She glanced at Mrs. Pierce, whose watery eyes didn't quite go with the huge smile on her face. Nova returned focus to her chocolate astronaut ice cream square and the lesson. Stephanie continued asking questions and giving facts about space travel, the upcoming mission, and the *Challenger.*

"In addition to launching the first American woman, *Challenger* was the vehicle that sent to space the first-ever African-American astronaut, Guion Stewart Bluford, Jr. One of the women going up today worked right here in New Hampshire before she joined NASA. Does anyone know what Christa McAuliffe's other job was?"

Nova did, of course, but Quiet Mary-Beth was the first to raise her hand.

"Teacher," she whispered once called on. She accepted a pink square of astronaut ice cream with a quiet "Thankth."

"You got it! *Challenger* is special for a lot of reasons. It was the first orbiter to land at Kennedy Space Center!" Stephanie tapped one of the newspaper articles. "Today it will take off for time number ten and it will return to Earth after one hundred forty-four hours and thirty-four minutes, or about six days."

Nova puffed out her chest a little. She didn't already know *all* of the information Stephanie was sharing, but she knew that.

Stephanie asked more questions, some super-hard, some super-simple, until everyone had a piece of ice cream except Margot, who ate through a tube and earned a Saturn sticker instead.

Finally, Mrs. Pierce thanked Stephanie, gave her a hug, and told everyone to stand and stretch—it was time to head to the other classrooms to watch the launch on CNN.

Nova hummed louder and louder and flapped harder and harder on her way down the hall as she mentally counted down all of the things that had made her morning perfect.

Ten: Billy helped her cut out a picture of the seven astronauts from the newspaper.

Nine: Francine said the sun was shining in Florida, which meant no more delays.

Eight: She was wearing her best launch outfit.

Seven: She'd held up Margot's head and made her laugh.

Six: NASA Bear smelled good because he'd gotten washed while she was sleeping.

Five: Now she had five friends: Mallory, Alex, Mary-Beth, Buddy, and Margot.

Four: Stephanie told everyone she was a space expert.

Three: She'd been able to answer a question *and* a bonus question about Sally Ride.

Two: She was about to see Christa McAuliffe become the First Teacher in Space.

One: Bridget was on her way. She'd promised.

Nova wasn't sure which of the ten things had her most excited.

Wait.

Yes, she was.

Seeing Bridget again.

That was the most exciting.

But it was close.

JAN 28, 1986

Dear Bridget,

T-minus zero days until *Challenger* launch.

    I am at school. It is almost time. I am waiting for you. Miss Chambers, Mallory, Mary-Beth, and me are watching the television in Mr. O'Reilly's class. Jefferson Middle School, first floor, sixth-grade wing, room 106, past the *Bridge to Terabithia* poster, just like I told you.

    Mr. O'Reilly has a brand-new digital clock, which is good because I need to know the time and it is too hard with the regular round clocks.

    It is 11:15 now.

    Do not be late.

    I am wearing my One Small Step T-shirt over the blue long-sleeved shirt with silver dots that look like stars and your old Neptune-colored mood ring. I picked this outfit out special. I wish I had a Cornflower blue NASA jacket like Christa McAuliffe and Ronald McNair.

    It is 11:21.

    NASA Bear is ready too. He is wearing his plastic bubble helmet and white NASA T-shirt, like always. He says he feels very excited but also nervous because he thinks you might be late even though I told him you would not miss it for all the planets in the solar system.

You promised.

It is 11:25.

You are still not here. Now I am starting to get nervous too.

The space shuttle *Challenger* looks like a toy, like the toy model in Christa McAuliffe's newspaper picture. A white cylinder with long wings to the sides, wings that jut out into triangles at the bottom, it is hoisted up on a tall brown tower with a tip like a bullet and two smaller white same-tipped silos on the sides. On the left wing is the American flag under the letters USA in black. On the right, the NASA logo, same as the one on NASA Bear's T-shirt, with the word *Challenger* under it. It's beautiful, exactly as I'd hoped it would look, like the one you've drawn for me so many times, with VEZINA where it should say NASA and *NovaBridge* instead of *Challenger*.

11:29.

It is hard to keep my body still but I know if I move too much Miss Chambers will squeeze my shoulders and say "Calm Body," which I hate. My thighs twitch, itching to bounce. Maybe it is okay if I rock just a little.

11:32.

You are going to miss it, Bridget.

Very very very soon, the astronauts will be rocketed into space and *you are going to miss it.*

I am writing it all down so you will know exactly what happened.

The TV screen is fuzzy. Static.

Mr. O'Reilly bangs his hand on the side.

The picture comes back into focus.

"That's all we need," he says, moving back to sit on the edge of his desk. "CNN in every classroom and our old set goes on the blink!"

"Say it ain't so!" cries a blond boy named Jeremiah, who is sitting front and center. Mallory calls him the class clown. He puts his hands over his heart and falls out of his chair. Some of the boys laugh. Mr. O'Reilly laughs too. I do not because it is not funny. Space is serious business.

Now I am filled with extra worries. What if the television stops working? I will miss the launch. And if you do not get here soon, you will miss it too, and then neither of us will have seen what we've been waiting for all this time.

"Isn't this exciting, Nova?" asks Miss Chambers. "Your foster mom says you love this stuff."

She has no idea.

My thighs bounce. I cannot stop them. I hear a

high-pitched noise, like the whine of a puppy. It happens again four more times before I realize it is coming from me. It is a new noise. I cannot stay still. I am a volcano, about to erupt, but not angry. The lava filling me from my toes to my nose is not angry. It is nervous, happy lava. Excited lava. Overwhelmed.

"Let's try taking deep breaths, Nova," says Miss Chambers. But I do not want to take deep breaths. I want to watch *Challenger* launch. I want you to watch it with me. I do not want you to miss it.

"Deep breaths, Nova," says Miss Chambers again. I cover my ears to block out her voice.

11:35.

11:36.

11:37.

WHERE ARE YOU, BRIDGET?

It's time.

Chapter Twelve

The class counted down together out loud.

"Ten, nine, eight, seven, six . . ."

"We have main engines start," said the TV announcer. Nova glanced toward the classroom door. It would open, Bridget would run in, and they'd watch together because she promised.

She promised.

But the door did not open.

". . . four, three, two, one . . ."

Nova drew her eyes back to the television at the front of the classroom without a second to spare. She focused on the bottom of the shuttle, where the fire burned.

Lift-off.

Thick white clouds like marshmallow fluff billowed up around the bottom of the space shuttle, from which a thick line of orange-yellow fire trailed. Birds, black dots against a gray-blue sky, flew off in all directions as the space shuttle shot up, attached to the reddish-brown bullet-shaped launcher. *Challenger* cleared the tower. It rose higher and higher into the sky, each second closer to the outer edges of Earth's atmosphere.

On the ground, crowds cheered and took pictures.

"Three engines running normally," the TV announcer said. Fire continued to follow the shuttle, like the tail of a zooming comet. Now that sky in the background was darker blue, true blue, like Francine's eyes.

"That voice belongs to Public Affairs Officer Steve Nesbitt," explained Mr. O'Reilly. Several students wrote that down to add to their postlaunch reports. Nova didn't. She would remember. She would remember every moment, every detail. She had to.

Someone would have to tell Bridget.

A trail of fire, cloud, and smoke continued to follow the space shuttle like the tail of a flying comet. One minute had passed since lift-off.

"So the twenty-fifth space shuttle mission is now on the way, after more delays than NASA cares to count . . . ," the announcer was saying. The screen identified him as Tom Mintier, CNN Correspondent.

They were doing it! They were headed into outer space! Unable to control herself, Nova hopped from her seat, flapping and squeaking and ignoring Miss Chambers, who was saying "Sit down, please! Take deep breaths!" It was too exciting for sitting. It was too exciting for deep breaths. Up it went. Up and up and up, closer to the sun, closer to the stars. Up and up and up . . .

Mintier continued, "This morning it looked like they were not going to be able to get off—"

Then one minute, thirteen seconds after lift-off.

It exploded.

The *Challenger* exploded.

Nova dropped NASA Bear. She clutched her hands.

On the screen, fire and debris flew out from the spacecraft in all directions.

No.

No, it couldn't have.

But it did.

The smoke resembled the Little Prince's snake after he ate the elephant, a thin white line split in two for the mouth at the top, a long winding tail at the bottom, with a round ball above the center, where Nova could almost picture the elephant rolling his eye to the sky.

Oh, great. I've been eaten.

"Looks like a couple of solid rocket boosters, uh, blew away from the side of the shuttle in an explosion," said the CNN correspondent.

A fireball in the sky, with pieces of debris clouded by multiple smoke trails rocketing out from all sides, was all that was left to be seen of the space shuttle. A solid gray mass detached from the side. The astronauts' pod? It whirled away. Gone.

There were no other signs of the *Challenger* on the screen. It had broken up into a cloud of smoke.

The camera swung away.

"Obviously a major malfunction," said the NASA announcer.

On the ground, the crowd gasped.

In the classroom, the students gasped.

The television cut to the faces of Christa McAuliffe's parents, then to the schoolchildren behind them. Kids like them. They didn't seem sad yet. They seemed confused.

Nova couldn't breathe. How could anybody?

"About forty-five seconds ago, a huge fireball in the sky . . . ," said the voice on TV.

Like shooting stars, streaks of smoke rained down from the shuttle toward the earth, bright white against a denim-blue sky. Nova could almost see the cloud of smoke above her head. She could almost smell ash descending from the atmosphere. She could almost feel the crisp air against her arms. She shivered in her ONE SMALL STEP shirt. It was as if she was there in Florida on the bleachers, staring in shock at the devastation in the sky, instead of sitting safely in her classroom watching it on CNN.

"We have the report from the flight dynamics officer that the vehicle has exploded," said the voice on the television. "We are checking with the recovery forces to see what can be done at this point."

"Ah dun," whispered Nova.

"Nova?" Miss Chambers placed a gentle hand on Nova's arm, but Nova pulled away. "Nova, honey, did you say something?"

Nova shook her head. She had nothing to say. Nothing could be done. Nothing was left. Nothing was left to hope for.

Oh, Bridget.

You and me and NASA Bear, our space shuttle, and the moon.

"No word yet on if there are any survivors," said the other announcer. Nova clenched her fists.

"Do you think it's possible?" whispered Class Clown Jeremiah. "Do you think it's possible they're alive?"

Mr. O'Reilly was shaking his head. "I'm . . . I'm so sorry, kids." His voice was quaking. "I'm sure there were no survivors. I'm so sorry."

Of course there were no survivors, thought Nova. Chal-lenger *was destroyed.*

Two minutes postexplosion.

Two minutes, thirty.

Two forty-five.

"Point of impact in the water," said the voice on the television.

Nova shook her head one-two-three-four times, try-ing to stop the movie screen in her mind from replay-ing the explosion over and over and over again, but it didn't work.

"Maybe they escaped?" suggested Julia. "Maybe they had parachutes?"

Mr. O'Reilly shook his head.

"Even if the seven astronauts somehow managed to survive the initial blast and breakup of the spacecraft, a person cannot hit the ocean going over two hundred miles per hour after a sixty-five-thousand-foot fall and live," Mr. O'Reilly said in a serious voice. "There's no way. It's not possible. I'm so sorry, kids. They'll try to recover the . . . the astronauts . . . from the water, but I'm afraid they're all gone."

"They're gone forever." Mallory's voice was quieter than Quiet Mary-Beth's and she was crying. "They'll never come back. They'll never go home. They'll never . . . they'll never . . ."

Miss Chambers moved to put her arms around shaking, sobbing Mallory. The rest of the class was silent, watching, not moving. Nova's body was frozen too, but her mind raced as she stared at the television, trying to understand what she'd just seen. This would not be like when Luke Skywalker flew from G.I. Joe's helicopter and landed on the floor. This was real life.

In real life, all seven astronauts were gone.

Forever.

And where was Bridget?

She hadn't come. She wasn't there like she'd promised.

On television, people in Florida were crying.

All around Nova, students were crying.

Mallory was crying. Mary-Beth was crying. Jeremiah and Julia and Zach were crying.

Miss Chambers was crying. Mr. O'Reilly was crying. Nova was not crying.

Nova had no tears to cry. Her tears were lost, somewhere inside her. Lost like she'd been her entire life. Lost in her own head, lost in her own world. Lost in space. Lost without Bridget.

And then, she knew.

She knew exactly where Bridget was. Bridget was in the same place she'd been when Nova last saw her.

Bridget wasn't coming for Nova. Bridget wasn't coming back.

So Nova would go to her.

Nova grabbed NASA Bear and took off running. She ran from the classroom. She ran down the hallway. She was almost to the front door when she heard Miss Chambers behind her.

"Nova, stop!"

But she could not stop. She needed to find Bridget. She needed to tell her what had happened. She needed them to suffer through it together, as they had through the last twelve years, holding hands, a big sister and her shadow, knowing nothing could hurt them, not really, so long as they were together.

The sound of Miss Chambers's heels clacked down

the hall after her, but Nova was fast and she'd had a head start. She was out the door.

"NOVA!"

Through the faculty parking lot, across the grassy baseball field, and all the way to the road.

She knew where to go. She'd get there. Running.

The scene played over and over again in her mind. She could not stop it. Countdown. Lift-off. One minute. One minute, ten seconds. One minute, twelve seconds. One minute, thirteen. Unlucky thirteen.

Countdown.

Lift-off.

Up.

Explosion.

Down.

Impact.

Over.

JAN 28, 1986

Dear Bridget,

I am writing this letter to you in my head because I am
running. I am running to find you because I know where
you are. I know you are in the place I last saw you, but
I thought you would not be there anymore. I thought
you would come find me. I thought we would watch
the *Challenger* launch together like you promised. You
promised!

I believed you. All these weeks since we ran away, I have
been waiting. But now I know. I know that you lied. You
are not coming back. You were never coming back. You
were never going to watch the *Challenger* launch with me.
You were never going to watch the First Teacher in Space
achieve our dream. I had to watch without you.

I had to watch the countdown and the lift-off and the
explosion.

I had to watch the fire and the dust and the smoke and
the small gray pod falling from the sky.

I had to watch them fail to leave the Earth's
atmosphere, fail to reach the stars.

They won't make it back, Bridget. They're gone. Forever.

You won't make it back either.

And I know why.

I remember.

Do you remember? As I run, the leafless trees rush by in a blur.

As I run, I see it all.

And as I run, I understand.

It started in the afternoon, the fight you had with our foster parents. They wanted you to stop seeing that boy. They wanted you to stop listening to music and getting bad grades and "acting out." That's what they kept saying. "You need to stop acting out, young lady!"

You said two words to them that I hadn't heard you say since you told off my teacher on the first day of kindergarten. Foster Mother slapped your face.

"That's it!" said Foster Father. "We're calling Mrs. Steele in the morning. Nova can go back to the group home and if they're smart they'll stick you in a juvenile detention center somewhere!"

You yelled back with more bad words. That's how I knew how mad you were. Then you took the stairs two at a time to our room and slammed the door.

That night, as soon as they were in bed, you woke me up, dressed me, and told me to be quiet. We were going to the house from the Halloween party. You had a plan.

The next thing I remember, I was sitting in the backseat of your boyfriend's car. I rocked back and forth and made my humming noise. You buckled my seat belt and kissed my temple and told me to quit worrying. Then you moved my tapping fingers away from my chin. You said, "Be happy, Nova! This is it! Our escape! From here to the moon, just you and me and NASA Bear, our space shuttle, and the moon!"

But it wasn't just us. It was us and your boyfriend too.

You promised we were going to be free.

Unless we got separated. Then you'd come back for me. That is what you said.

"Our planet is in order, little sister! Let's go rake out our active volcanoes!" You borrowed those lines from *The Little Prince.*

"Oh-kay, Bidge." I trusted you. I pointed to the sky. It was dark. The moon was bright against a black sky. The stars were twinkling. My favorite kind of night. Yours too. I smiled. You smiled.

"Let the stars be not our tiny lights, but our guides!" You borrowed that line too, except it is really "For the travelers the stars are guides. For others they are nothing but tiny lights."

"What are you talking about?" asked your boyfriend, the one Mrs. Steele called a bad influence. He was twirling silver keys on a ring around his index finger, smiling.

"It's a sister thing," you said. He shrugged. You laughed. He got into the driver's seat. You sat in front, beside him, as usual, but I wanted you in the back, with me. He put one hand on the wheel and turned the key in the ignition with the other.

My seat was directly behind yours. I reached out to touch your hair but you pulled away, turning to look at me, sitting on your knees with your back to the windshield. You were not wearing a seat belt. Your boyfriend was not wearing a seat belt. Only I wore a seat belt.

"This is our escape! No more foster homes, Super Nova. No more getting moved around and split up and then put back together until they send us away again. We don't need any more temporary parents pretending like they'll be forever families. I've always taken care of you, right?"

"Mm."

"And I always will. No matter what happens, we'll be okay, okay? Child Services, if they find us, they're gonna be mad . . . maybe so mad they split us up for good. But if they do take you away, I promise I'll come back for you. I'll be back for the launch and I'll be back again when I turn eighteen in August, so I can take you away. Don't worry. I promise."

I was still worried but I said "Oh-kay" to make you happy.

Leaning into the back, you reached into your old backpack, which was on the floor between my feet, and pulled out NASA Bear. You handed him to me. "He's completely yours now, Nova. Take care of him."

I felt confused but you laughed, kissed your fingers, and tapped my nose to give me the kiss.

"By the year 2000, people will be headed to space all the time! On vacation, like it's Disneyland or Myrtle Beach. Parents will go, 'Say, honey, what should we do this summer? Visit Auntie Em and Uncle Henry down in Kansas, or take the kids to the moon again?' Kids will be like so over boring rocket ships they'll pick Kansas for the scenery change! You and I can take NASA Bear with us. He'll be the first astronaut teddy in space. It'll be glorious."

The boy in the driver's seat laughed. "What? You're crazy, babe." You giggled even though he called you a not-nice name—crazy. You kissed his cheek. My own cheeks burned. Why did you kiss him?

"You like music, right, Nova?" He turned on the radio. "This is the sixties and seventies station. Maybe they'll play David Bowie for you!"

I liked the radio station but I did not like him, I did not like how he was taking up all your time and making you forget about me, so I did not say "Mm."

He drove very fast. Snow-coated trees whirled by, making me dizzy. I never liked being in cars. Will it feel this way in a rocket ship too? Will I get space-sick the way I get carsick? Probably not, since roller coasters are more like rocket ships than cars are and I don't get sick on them. I hugged NASA Bear close and tried not to think about it. I wanted to tap my fingers against my chin but I knew you did not want me to worry and I wanted you to be happy with me.

The radio was loud. Too loud. I pressed one ear against my shoulder so I had a free hand to hug NASA Bear. In the front seat, you were talking and laughing but I could not hear your words. You opened your window and more sound whooshed in. You sat on the door, putting the top half of your body outside the car, your legs on the inside. That was not safe. I wanted to scream at you, Bridget. I wished I could talk so I could scream, "That is not safe!" I opened my mouth but no sounds come out.

The boy grabbed your arm. He pulled you back inside. He said, "What're you doing? You have a death wish?" but he was laughing.

It started to snow but you did not put up the window.

I was cold. Most of the time I like cold, but not that night. I didn't have a coat.

He drove too fast. The music was too loud. You changed the radio station. The announcer said, "We're counting down the best songs of 1985! This is number nine: 'Crazy for You' by Madonna!"

The car slid a little on the icy road. Your boyfriend said "Whoa, major fishtail!" and laughed but I felt scared and sick.

"Bidge," I managed to say. "Bidge, no!"

You did not hear me. You were singing along with Madonna. You called Madonna "the best there is" like you'd forgotten all about David Bowie. I could not stay still or quiet anymore. I squeaked and hummed and rocked. The seat belt pressed against my twisted pretzel tummy when I rocked, which hurt, so I leaned forward, placing my head between my knees, pressing my fingers to my chin, cradling NASA Bear against my cheek.

Too fast. Too loud.

The car fishtailed again.

Your boyfriend said a bad word. You screamed.

The car spun around and around. It happened before I could lift my head.

Impact.

The front seat came into the backseat, slamming into my knees, pressing against the top of my head.

The roof came down with a crunch, stopping inches above me.

I could not lift my head.

I could not see you. I could not hear you.

I could not hear anything.

I closed my eyes.

Darkness.

When I felt arms around me, I woke up.

It was you, it had to be. You were carrying me back to the foster home to get my coat because I was cold. So cold.

I was still holding NASA Bear.

There was wetness on the side of my face. It ran from my hair into my mouth, tasting like metal.

Blood.

I wanted to touch it but my arms were too heavy. Too tired. Stuck.

"She's alive!" shouted a man. I opened one eye. The man was holding me, not you. "This little one's breathing! Get a stretcher!"

Bridget?

"There's a survivor!" exclaimed a woman's voice. Not yours.

It was still snowing but the winter air smelled like smoke.

I opened my eyes again. I saw a twisted block of metal,

the same color the car was, but it could not be the car. There was no hood, no room for an engine. No laughing boy with a leather jacket. No you.

I saw a long truck turned over. The truck was on fire. The flames raged high. Ash fell onto my face. Ash, like from a volcano.

So many loud noises surrounded me. Shouting, sirens, the crackling of the fire. I wanted to cover my ears but I could not move.

Then I was on a bed. The bed was on wheels. Strangers strapped me down.

An ambulance. I was in an ambulance. The siren was screaming. I hate screaming even more than I hate crying.

I knew where we were going. To a hospital. That is where ambulances go. I still could not see you, couldn't hear you. Were you sitting in the front seat?

I fell asleep.

When I woke again, I was in a hospital room. I looked around. NASA Bear was on the table beside my bed. He was clean and his fur was fluffed, like someone gave him a bath.

My body ached, my brain hurt.

There were people talking softly in the hall. I recognized the voice of Mrs. Steele, our social worker. She must have known where you were.

"She won't be able to answer your questions," she was saying. "She only says a couple of words. She can't read or write. She's autistic, nonverbal, and severely mentally retarded."

I waited for you to start hollering at her, the way you always did when someone called me the R-word. But maybe you were asleep in your own hospital room, because nobody said, "My sister's not dumb. She's a thinker, not a talker."

"We have to know what happened." It was the voice of a man, a voice I never heard before. "She's the sole survivor of the crash."

"I'm sorry, Officer," said Mrs. Steele. "She can't speak to you."

Sole survivor?

I didn't know it then, but *sole* means only. One. Alone.

A lone survivor. Only one.

But that could not be true.

Because you were in the crash too.

And if we were both in the crash . . .

And there was only one survivor . . .

And I'm alive . . .

No.

They made a mistake.

We are going into space together! We are going to

soar past the stars, holding NASA Bear between us! We are going to vacation on Venus, to meet Martians on Mars! We are going to leave footprints on the moon!

* * *

I have arrived.

But you are gone.

And I am alone.

I drop to my knees on the side of the road. How long have I been running?

Francine and I have passed this point many times when she takes the long way home from school. Sometimes she points it out and asks how I feel. I close my eyes and push her words away from my ears.

But now, here I am.

For the first time since the accident, I look around.

There are no tire marks in the street. There is no sign of the twisted metal or the burning truck. No snow. No ice.

There is only a mound of frozen dirt on the side of the road and a white wooden cross. The cross Joanie showed me after we had pancakes at the diner.

And now I understand.

Here is where you are, Bridget.

Here is where you ended.

The point of impact.

The ocean.

Our Sea of Tranquility.

I lie down beside the cross. I rest my head on NASA Bear.

You were not there, Bridget. You broke your promise.

We were supposed to watch the *Challenger* launch together.

We were supposed to watch them send up the First Teacher in Space.

You were supposed to be there when I watched the *Challenger* lift-off.

You were supposed to be there when I watched the *Challenger* explode.

But you were not there. Because you are here.

I do not know why I did not understand it before. Mrs. Steele told me what happened to you. Francine and Billy told me. Joanie told me.

But you promised to come back and you always keep your promises, so I guess I thought that death is not forever. That your promise must be stronger than dying. Because you have always been stronger than me, even though I was the sole survivor.

I did not understand it, Bridget, until I saw the *Challenger* explode, but now I do. Now I know sometimes what we want doesn't matter.

Sometimes people can't keep their promises.

Sometimes even astronauts can't reach the stars.

I did not understand it before, Bridget, but I understand it now.

Can you hear me, Major Tom?
Can you ...?
Planet Earth is blue—
And there's nothing I can do.

I can feel your arms around me, Bridget.

I can hear your heartbeat in my ear.

I know that I am not alone.

It's still you and me and NASA Bear, our space shuttle, and the moon.

You didn't come find me.

So I've found you.

Chapter Thirteen

Francine pulled over on the side of the road. She ran from the car, followed by Miss Chambers.

"Nova?" Francine reached Nova first, curled up on her side next to the wooden cross, hands over her ears, eyes closed. Francine dropped to her knees and cradled Nova's head against her chest.

Nova could feel a heartbeat thumping in her ear.

Bridget?

No.

Her eyes fluttered open. Her head felt heavy.

"We need to get her warm," said Francine. "She's been outside with no coat. She's freezing." She took off her own coat and wrapped Nova in it. With help from Miss Chambers, she picked Nova up and carried her to the car. Francine placed her gently in the backseat and Miss Chambers covered her with her own coat like a blanket. They got back into the car.

Francine turned her key in the ignition.

Nova closed her eyes. She wanted to sleep.

* * *

When Nova opened her eyes again, she was back in the too-big bedroom.

She could smell chicken soup and Francine's perfume.

For a few seconds, she felt confused. Then it all came crashing back.

The conversation between Mrs. Steele and the police officer in the hospital hallway.

Being handed the box of her sister's things.

Driving to a new foster home.

Meeting Billy and Francine.

Realizing they were the same people who'd been to visit her when she was in the hospital. When Francine read Dr. Seuss. When Billy brought brownies.

She'd been in the hospital during the funerals.

Now she was home, with Francine sitting beside her bed and Billy standing in the doorway. It was just like the day they met, except Francine was not holding a book. She stroked Nova's hair instead.

"She's awake," whispered Francine.

"You gave us quite a scare," said Billy. He held up the soup bowl. "Are you hungry?"

Nova sat up against the headboard. She was a little hungry.

"We thought this would be such a wonderful day for you," said Francine as Billy placed the bowl on the bedside table. He sat on top of the wooden toy box.

"We know how much you'd been looking forward to the launch, Nova. We can't tell you how sorry we are. . . ." Francine's voice cracked.

"Everything's going to be fine, Nova," said Billy. "Have some soup."

Francine held the bowl so she could spoon some into Nova's mouth. Just as Nova had guessed, it was chicken noodle.

Billy blew his nose into a tissue.

"We were so worried about you," he said. "Us, Joanie, Mrs. Pierce, Miss Chambers, Mr. O'Reilly . . . Don't ever, *ever* disappear on us like that again, Nova. Don't ever run away. Don't leave school without me or Francine or Mrs. Steele. Never again. Promise us."

Nova looked from his face to Francine's. They both looked like they'd been crying. Francine set the spoon back in the bowl.

Why were they crying?

"Please promise us you won't run away like that ever again," said Francine softly.

"Ah," said Nova. She nodded. "Mm."

For some reason, this made Francine cry more.

"It's nice to hear you talk," explained Billy. If it was nice, why was Francine crying?

"We were going to tell you tonight. Well, ask you, really," said Francine. "After dinner, during dessert. Billy already made cheesecake."

Nova wrinkled up her eyebrows. *Ask what?*

"We think you've been moved around too much, Nova." Billy was smiling now, but Francine was still sniffling. "You've had eleven homes in seven years. That's not right."

"We'd been thinking about becoming foster parents for a while." Francine wiped her eyes and reached for the bowl again. She fed Nova like she was a baby, but Nova didn't mind.

"Our kids are adults and we're grandparents now," said Billy. "But we felt like we could still be parents too. So we decided to become foster parents."

"That's right," said Francine. "Then, when we read about Bridget in the paper . . . when we read about *you* . . . We thought it seemed like fate."

There was that word again. *Fate.* Nova wished she could talk so she could ask what it meant. She guided Francine's hands, which were holding the bowl, toward the bedside table. She wasn't hungry anymore.

"You survived," Billy said. "And you needed a family."

"We want to be that family," said Francine. "That's what we were going to ask you after dinner."

"Forever," clarified Billy.

Francine moved from the chair to the edge of Nova's bed. "Right. Not for just a little while, not as foster parents, but forever. We want to adopt you, Nova."

"Today was supposed to be such a happy day." Billy took Francine's place in the chair. He reached for Nova's hand and gave it a squeeze. "We had a whole speech about reaching for the stars, following dreams—"

Francine cut him off. "We've loved you since the first day we sat with you in the hospital, reading while you slept. We wanted to start the adoption process then, but . . ."

"But Mrs. Steele said we needed to foster you for a while first. I know it hasn't been that long, but I think we're doing fine."

Nova smiled. She liked how Billy and Francine were always finishing each other's sentences.

"Our sons can't wait to meet you," said Billy. "Joanie's told them a lot about you. She loves having a little sister. And our grandsons, they're so excited. I know they're going to love you as much as we do."

Francine leaned closer, stroking Nova's hair again. "Would you like that? I know you can understand me. I can tell. If you could . . . if you could nod, or say 'okay,' if you want . . . if you want us to adopt you . . . if you want to be part of our family . . . if that would be . . . if that would make you happy . . . could you tell us?"

Nova moved Francine's hand away, then pulled her other hand away from Billy. She sat up as much as possible, propped on her elbows. She thought it over.

"Ah."

She was finally going to have a forever family. For real.

She wondered what Bridget would think.

"Ah?" asked Francine. "Does that mean . . ."

"We can adopt you?" asked Billy. "It's okay?"

Nova carefully made eye contact, first with Francine's Midnight Blue eyes, next with Billy's Raw Umber ones. Then she looked away because she did not like looking into people's eyes.

But in her clearest voice, she said, "Oh-kay."

SUPERNOVA

FEB 1, 1986

Dear Bridget,

It has been four days since the *Challenger* disaster. Since
I understood that you are not coming back. Since the
Wests asked to adopt me. I have not gone back to school.
I've been here at home with my future forever family and
NASA Bear, thinking.

And talking.

Sometimes I talk out loud, like I used to talk to you,
and Billy and Francine try to understand but it's hard. So
for the last three days, Francine has been writing words
and drawing pictures for me. She keeps them all in a
special spiral notebook with a Crayola Goldenrod sun
on the front cover. She made a page for food, a page for
books, a page for family, a page for friends, a page for
places, a page for space, and two pages just for school.
(NASA Bear is on the space page, not the family page,
but that's okay.) Francine says Mrs. Pierce is going to work
with me on communication a lot when I go back, and
Miss Chambers will too, but it's hard to talk without you.

It's hard knowing I will never talk to you again.

Yesterday, Billy and Francine took me back to the white cross on the side of the road. We painted your name on it together, with Francine's hand over my hand holding the brush. Then Billy helped me bury a tin box full of the letters I have written you in the last two weeks, except for this one. This one I will keep with me. We also put the stolen Little People astronaut in there and a newspaper clipping about the *Challenger* disaster.

I am keeping the tape you made, the one with "Space Oddity."

I will still be an astronaut, Bridget. I know it has only been four days since the explosion and Billy says we can't know what's next for the space program, but I believe they will send astronauts up again. I'll be with them, someday. Maybe not on a vacation trip to the moon, like how people go to Disneyland and Myrtle Beach, because space is serious business. But maybe I will be the First Autistic Girl in Space.

Francine says I can do anything. She says I am smart and brave.

She also says you can still see me, so I should try to make you proud.

I like to think you are already in space, waiting for me. When I am old and I die, I'll join you on our secret planet, like the Little Prince, where together we will rake out our active volcanoes.

Last night, Francine looked up *nova* in the book from my astronomy class. It turns out a nova is not an explosion at the end of a star's life, like a supernova. A nova is an explosion on a white dwarf that makes a dull star get brighter and brighter all of a sudden until it is the brightest thing in the sky after the sun and moon, but then it fades back to normal. A supernova kills a star, but not a nova. In a nova, the star survives the explosion.

That's me, Bridget.

I survived.

You are gone.

But I'll go on.

I miss you.

Love,
Nova

Author's Note

The *Challenger* launch was not originally scheduled to be Tuesday, January 28, as it is in the book. In reality, the launch date was postponed several times. The morning of the launch, some of those working on the mission believed it was too cold to proceed, but since there had already been multiple delays, NASA decided to go on despite the warnings. NBC (airing live from Los Angeles) reported that icicles had formed on the shuttle but were presumed to have broken off upon lift-off. Just before the explosion, the news announcer said the astronauts would "check on (the icicle situation) later."

A few crew members working on the launch weren't sure *Challenger* would even take off. They rejoiced when the shuttle "made it," but 73 seconds after takeoff, the craft broke apart. Though announcers and TV viewers thought it had exploded, people watching from the ground heard not a boom but silence as the engines stopped running. The shuttle's fuel tank tore apart, which is what caused the huge fireball and smoke. The cause of the disaster was found primarily to be the failure of two rubber O-rings that had been used to separate sections of the rocket booster. Both O-rings failed due to cold, which means the accident was not only preventable, but something NASA experts had worried about prior to launch.

The tragedy aired on live television and was seen by children in many school classrooms like Nova's.

* * *

*"Sometimes when we reach for the stars,
we fall short, but we must pick ourselves up again and
press on despite the pain. . . . We can find consolation
only in faith, for we know in our heart that
you who flew so high, and so proud,
will make your home beyond the stars."*

—President Ronald Reagan
at the *Challenger* memorial service, February 1, 1986

The loss of the space shuttle *Challenger* halted the US space program for over two years, but in 2007, Barbara Morgan, who had been runner-up to Christa McAuliffe in the Educator Astronaut contest, became the first teacher in space. Morgan studied for nearly a decade after *Challenger* to become an astronaut. She was a standard Mission Specialist and licensed amateur radio operator. Three weeks after returning from her successful first trip into space, she told a group of students at Walt Disney World, "Reach for your dreams . . . the sky is no limit." Those words are now etched into a plaque on a wall of Mission: Space beside McAuliffe's quote, which begins, "Space is for everybody."

"Everybody" includes kids like Nova, who are autistic and

nonverbal. Many autistic people are nonverbal and therefore use other methods of communication. Unfortunately, for a long time, the options for nonverbal people were limited. Nowadays, a broader understanding of autism and much better technology have made it possible for someone like Nova to carry around a tablet or speech device that can help her speak to others by touching buttons, using pre-programmed words or pictures, or typing the words out. Many of these devices and programs feature small images called PECS (Picture Exchange Communication System) that can be used individually or to create sentences. American Sign Language or Signed Exact English are other possible communication methods for nonverbal people. These methods are great not only for nonverbal autistic children, but for people who struggle to communicate verbally for any reason, including those who have had strokes and those with Apraxia of Speech.

One misconception is that people who are nonverbal are also unable to understand what is being said to them, which is why a lot of adults in Nova's life have addressed her in loud voices with short, basic sentences. It is important to her that Bridget has never done that, nor does Francine. It is also important to Nova that people read novels to her, instead of the books with few words that she's used to getting from teachers. There are a lot of autistic middle schoolers who prefer chapter books to picture books, including kids like Nova who can't read them independently yet—not that there's anything wrong with loving picture books!

When Neil Armstrong stepped onto the moon in 1969,

he said, "That's one small step for a man, one giant leap for mankind." On the recording, the "a" is hard to hear, and as a result, his famous words are among the most misquoted of all time. I decided to have Bridget keep the "a" because she and Nova know how frustrating it is to be misunderstood.

Since the word "autism" was first used as a diagnosis over a century ago, the definition and criteria have changed considerably. When Nova was in school, much less was understood about autism, which had only been added to the Diagnostic and Statistical Manual of Mental Disorders (DSM) as an independent disorder in 1980. Some of what people believed at that time is now known to be incorrect. In 1991, the federal government made autism a Special Education category, which has helped more kids on the spectrum to be given a diagnosis and get the personalized education and assistive technology they need. When Nova was twelve, around one in 1,000 children in America were diagnosed with autism. As of 2018, thanks to an expanded criteria and better understanding, that number is around one in 45.

Nova has many sensory issues, which can make everyday life difficult, as sounds may be painful, clothing may be unbearably uncomfortable, and the textures of certain foods might cause anxiety. When Nova has her meltdown, it is because of a combination of emotional anguish and sensory overload; when she is upset, she has a more difficult time filtering out the agitating sounds around her. In 1986, it is possible that her reaction—hurting herself, screaming, flopping to the floor—would have been called a "fit" or "tantrum," but

I chose to have Francine identify it as a meltdown because I felt it was important for readers to understand that what Nova experienced was the result of being overstimulated and overwhelmed. It was not a tantrum.

One label that Bridget and Nova particularly dislike is "severely mentally retarded." The diagnosis "mental retardation" was originally brought into use to replace other hurtful labels like "idiocy" starting around 1895, but over time came to be harmful in its own right. By the 1960s, "retarded" was used as both a diagnostic term and as an insult, and the two uses continued to overlap for over forty years. When Nova was twelve, "mentally retarded" would have been one of her official diagnoses, while "retard" would have been a cruel name for another kid to call her, as Carrot Krystle does during Home Ec.

It has taken a long time for the "R-word" to be replaced. In 1992, the Association for Retarded Citizens of the United States changed its name to the Arc of the United States. In 2007, the American Association on Mental Retardation was renamed the American Association on Intellectual and Developmental Disabilities. In 2010, President Obama signed Rosa's Law, which mandated changing "mentally retarded" to "individuals with intellectual disabilities" within federal labor, health, and education documents. And finally, in 2013, the *Diagnostic and Statistical Manual of Mental Disorders (DSM-5)* was updated, reclassifying "mental retardation" as "intellectual disability," though other terms like "cognitively delayed" and "developmentally delayed" are also in use today.

When I was little, I was labeled "particular," "picky," and a "space cadet" because of my vast and varied sensory issues, obsessive-compulsive disorder, and overactive imagination. It was not until adulthood that I was told (initially by a board-certified behavior analyst) that these traits combined with others could indicate Asperger's, as the disorder often presents differently in girls than in boys (and had previously not been extensively studied in girls). When writing Nova, I based some of her spectrum behavior on myself, but I also made her nonverbal, a late reader, and unable to write, which greatly isolated her in the days before the electronic communication devices. Now, with the release of the *DSM-5,* which expanded the criteria for Autism Spectrum Disorder, Asperger's is no longer its own diagnosis.

A lot of what we know about space has changed since 1986 too. For example, when Nova was in school, there were nine planets, but in 2006, Pluto's status was downgraded, so today there are eight, and Neptune, which was thought to have two moons, actually has fourteen. We also have an International Space Station now, in which astronauts from the United States, Russia, Japan, and Europe continuously orbit the Earth, and in 2015 liquid water was discovered on Mars, though people can't vacation there . . . yet!

Acknowledgments

Writing a book is a little like traveling to the moon—in both cases, without your crew to help and guide you, you'll never get off the ground. I was therefore fortunate to have an amazing crew working with me to make *Planet Earth Is Blue* the best it could be.

At the start, there was Katy Loutzenhiser, my critique partner and author of *If You're Out There*. Thanks for meeting me at cafés all over Brooklyn to write, vent, and consume too much caffeine. For the years of encouragement, beta reading, and/or patiently listening, thank you to Jennifer Kuhn, Dean Kubota, Candace Rosas, Tonya Brock, and Kris Allard.

I wouldn't have been able to write much of anything without the support of my family. To my mom, Ann, for whom books are like Benadryl, thank you for almost making it through the whole first chapter before falling asleep and for sharing Book News with everyone in the Veterans of Foreign Wars Auxiliary. A thousand thanks also go to my dad, Tim (who wants me to write his book next), and my brother, Tyler (who fed my vicious kitten, Shakespeare, when I was away), plus Meme, Pepe, Grandma, Abi, Amelia, Deb, and

Loren. And to the seven incredible kids to whom this book is dedicated: a rainbow of emoji hearts.

To agent extraordinaire Katie Grimm, who said she cried *and* read the book in one sitting, I am so sorry for being so happy about making you cry! Thank you for helping me make Nova's story tighter and richer and better. I genuinely couldn't ask for—or imagine—a better agent.

My dream editor, as I told Katie, has long been Wendy Lamb, and I am beyond appreciative to Wendy and to assistant editor Dana Carey for their insight, inquiries, notes, and edits. The entire process has been incredible, and I am grateful to have had you both to work with (and guide me). Caroline Gertler and Sylvia Al-Mateen also made helpful suggestions.

Thank you to everyone at Wendy Lamb Books and Penguin Random House who helped bring *Planet Earth Is Blue* from a messy Word document to a real book, including designer Leslie Mechanic, cover artist Jungsuk Lee, reader Elena Meuse, and copy editors Barbara Perris, Colleen Fellingham, and Alison Kolani. For the use of lyrics from David Bowie's song "Space Oddity," thank you to Onward Music Ltd. in London and TRO Essex Music International, Inc., in New York.

I'm indebted to my early readers: Kathy Lundy, Lori Garrity, Amanda Pronovost, Jennifer John, Heather Craven, Alexa Dalpe, Steph Hebert, Amie Lynn Thompson, and Carolyn Hoye Hackett. I later turned the book over to tweens: Mackenzie Peloquin, Sophie Derman, and Meadow Sweet. Having them read Nova's story for the first time was scary and exciting. Thank you to Beth Kirkonnell for helping with Buddy's signs, and to my awesome PitchWars mentor, Ellie Terry, for helping me get *Planet Earth Is Blue* to a submission-worthy level. Through PitchWars, I was fortunate to connect with many incredible writers, including Cindy Baldwin, Amanda Rawson Hill, Helen Hoang, and Yael Mermelstein. Yael's class was present in Florida for the *Challenger* launch and she saw the disaster firsthand; her feedback was invaluable.

I am also ever-grateful for my wonderful sensitivity readers who read for authenticity purposes, and thankful to those who work in the autism field and offered their feedback and guidance, including Connecticut-certified pre-K–12 special education teacher Kris Allard, who has been working with autistic students for twenty-five years, and board-certified behavior analyst Dr. Bob Worsham, who supplied information about how kids on the spectrum were taught in public schools back in 1986. Lily Koblenz, MD, was also very helpful. Several of my draft readers also work in the field of special education or are on the autism spectrum themselves.

I'd have never dreamed of being an author if not for the fantabulous English/writing teachers I've had from grade six through grad school: Mr. Weigel, Mr. Moody, Ms. Waters, Ms. Karro-Gutierrez, Mr. Martin, Dr. Chibeau, Lisa Rowe Fraustino, Nancy Ruth Patterson, and Amanda Cockrell, *et merci à professeur de français Madame Rose pour* Le Petit Prince.

Last, I want to recognize and remember the seven astronauts on board the *Challenger* in 1986: Christa McAuliffe,

Dr. Ronald E. McNair, Dr. Judith A. Resnik, Francis R. Scobee, Gregory Jarvis, Ellison S. Onizuka, and Mike J. Smith, plus Dr. Sally K. Ride, who became the first American woman in space aboard *Challenger* in 1983 and later investigated the disaster.

> *"Space is for everybody."*
>
> —CHRISTA MCAULIFFE

About the Author

Nicole Panteleakos is a middle-grade author, playwright, and Ravenclaw whose plays have been performed at numerous theaters and schools in Connecticut and New York City. She earned her BA in theater scriptwriting from Eastern Connecticut State University and is working toward her MFA in children's literature at Hollins University.

Prior to Hollins, Nicole was an instructor in an autism school in Connecticut, where she focused on teaching creative writing and helping kids with limited speech communicate. She volunteered at an autism center's after-school program in Brooklyn, New York, worked at a weekend social program for NYC students on the spectrum, and did home care, including respite care for foster children. Though she based many of Nova's qualities and quirks on herself as a tween, she was also inspired by the amazing kids she has cared for, including three fantabulous godchildren.

She travels often and has a cat named Shakespeare. *Planet Earth is Blue* is her debut novel.

Visit Nicole on Twitter at @NicWritesBooks or on her website, nicolepanteleakos.com.